She held out her left hand to him. "Circumstances have changed."

He studied her bare hand for a moment. "I hope that had nothing to do with me."

She shook her head. "Christopher's family had a little problem with me being Ojibwa."

He pulled his brow down. "Why should that matter?"

Exactly. But it did. She waved her hand in dismissal. "It's a long story. And believe me rather boring. So does seven work for you?"

"I still don't know if it's a good idea."

"Why?"

He rubbed the back of his neck, and his pained expression said he was trying to find the words to say what he wanted to say as kindly as possible.

The stunned look he had given her when she had said she didn't attend church flashed before her. Was he that prejudiced that he couldn't even have dinner with someone who didn't believe as he did? "Is this because I don't hold the same religious beliefs as you?"

"Well, there is that, too."

"Too? So you want nothing to do with me because I'm not religious like you. Christopher doesn't want me because I'm part Native American. My stepfathers didn't want me because I wasn't theirs. Can't anyone accept me just as I am? Do I always have to change and be someone else to please others?"

"It's not like that."

She moved toward the door, but Will was standing in her way. "Let me go."

MARY DAVIS is a full-time writer whose first published novel was *Newlywed Games* from Multnomah. She enjoys going into schools and talking to kids about writing. Mary lives near Colorado's Rocky Mountains with her husband, three teens, and seven pets. Please visit her Web site at http://marydavisbooks.com.

Books by Mary Davis

HEARTSONG PRESENTS
HP399—Cinda's Surprise
HP436—Marty's Ride
HP514—Roger's Return
HP653—Lakeside
HP669—The Island
HP682—The Grand Hotel

Don't miss out on any of our super romances. Write to us at the following address for information on our newest releases and club information.

Heartsong Presents Readers' Service
PO Box 721
Uhrichsville, OH 44683

Or visit www.heartsongpresents.com

Heritage

Mary Davis

Heartsong Presents

To all those who were here first.

A note from the Author:
I love to hear from my readers! You may correspond with me by writing:

Mary Davis
Author Relations
PO Box 721
Uhrichsville, OH 44683

ISBN 1-59310-940-7

HERITAGE

Our mission is to publish and distribute inspirational products offering exceptional value and biblical encouragement to the masses.

Cover design by Jocelyne Bouchard

PRINTED IN THE U.S.A.

one

The problem with perfection is, there is no room for mistakes.

Rachel Coe gazed at her reflection in her freestanding full-length mirror, a gift from her fiancé. Her knee-length black evening dress was conservative where it needed to be but as feminine as Christopher liked it. She turned once, slowly, to make sure there were no spots or wrinkles.

She didn't want him to find any flaws. If she presented herself as perfect, then Christopher's family could have no objections, and she would be included. She would belong to a family with a background. . .a heritage.

She studied her dress again. Christopher hadn't seen this dress yet, but she was fairly confident he would approve. If not, she could quickly change into one of her other black dresses. She didn't want to depend on him for everything, but she valued his advice. There were subtle nuances on what was acceptable to wear, do, and say in the circles in which his family moved—nuances she was still getting the hang of. This dress would be her self-test on how she was doing.

She put on a short string of pearls and the matching earrings Christopher's mother, Emma, had given her as an engagement present. They had belonged to Emma's mother. She fingered them at her throat. Something from the past. Something from bygone days to hold onto. Something to pass on to her children. *A heritage.*

The Winstons could trace their ancestors back to the founding fathers of Boston. So they said. Rachel's own mother had moved to the area and married a good and decent man when Rachel was just a baby, but they were always on the fringes of society, the society that mattered, anyway. Now she was about to step over the line that separated one segment of society from another. A step up. She could only trace her roots back as far as her mother, and she didn't even know where her mother had come from.

Her stepfather died when she was thirteen, and her mother remarried twice more, pounding into Rachel's head that if she didn't have her looks, she didn't have anything. When her mother became terminally ill and lost her hair from chemo, Rachel's third stepfather walked out on them. The rat.

The doorbell rang. She sucked in a quick breath. Christopher. She glanced at the clock on the wall. He was early. Trying to catch her imperfect? She ran Sunset Rose over her lips, his favorite color on her. It complimented her olive skin. She checked herself in the mirror by the front door of her upscale apartment and touched her dark brown hair. Perfect. She swung the door open.

A deliveryman thrust a clipboard toward her. "Sign on line seventeen." She heaved a small sigh of relief at it not being Christopher, even though she was ready. She didn't like to feel rushed when greeting him. She didn't want him to sense her being flustered. If she acted and dressed as they did, they would think she belonged, even if she knew better. After signing, he handed her a large registered express envelope and left.

She turned over the delivery. *Jacobson and Son, Attorneys at Law.* This wasn't Christopher's family's attorney. She pulled the tab to rip open the cardboard envelope and pulled out a business-sized envelope.

The doorbell rang, and she jumped. Showtime. She dropped the two envelopes on the entry table then checked her appearance as she took a calming breath. Just as she reached for the knob the envelopes registered. *Never leave personal items out in the open.* She grabbed them both and threw them in the bottom of her entry closet.

She stepped back as she opened the door so Christopher could see her full appearance in one—hopefully approving— glance. Christopher scanned her from head to toe as he stepped inside and closed the door. He wore a black tux and a lock of his thick wavy hair hung down on his forehead. He combed it back with his fingers. "Is that a new dress?"

"I bought it yesterday." She turned slowly for him and held her breath. "Do you like it?"

He walked up to her and took her hands, holding them out from her and assessing the dress. "You picked this out all on your own?"

She nodded, daring to breathe. Did he like it or not?

He nodded and smiled. "You have certainly improved your eye for fashion. Who designed it?"

She named the designer. She knew that was important. Being a model she had worn the fashions of all the top designers, but in her personal life she saw no point in indulging in their high price tags. . .until Christopher entered her life. Now she found herself worrying about what she wore whenever she expected Christopher or was going out in public where someone might recognize her as a future Winston.

"Then it's perfect. You look perfect." Perfection was not easy to come by. . .and so easy to lose. "And Grandmother's pearls are just the right touch. In fact, you look so good, I might just stay here with you and skip Mother's party." He pulled her close and kissed her.

As tempting as that might be, she knew he'd never let down his mother by at least not putting in an appearance at one of her parties. It's where she'd met Christopher. She'd gone with Mark, a photographer from the modeling agency. Christopher hadn't seemed interested in her, and he certainly hadn't interested her, but he called the agency the following Monday. She overlooked his fair hair and pale eyes and focused on his height and charm. At five foot nine, she intimidated some men, especially when she wore heels, but Christopher topped six feet and preferred her in heels.

He stepped back from her and smiled then ran a thumb along her bottom lip. "I smeared your lipstick. Sorry about that."

She put her hand to her lip. His roguish smile told her he wasn't really sorry. "I'll go fix it."

✿

Rachel sipped her lemon water while everyone else at the Winstons' large dining table drank red wine. She had never acquired a taste for it. Her mother had also drilled into her head from a young age that alcohol would only make her look prematurely old. Whether that was true or not, she saw no point in risking it for something that only impaired one's faculties. When most people had had a few drinks they either became loud, rude, or obnoxious. Usually all three. Their inhibitions and senses dulled. She always wanted to be in control of what she was doing.

Mr. Winston set down his glass. "Christopher's namesake came over on the Mayflower."

Of that her future father-in-law was proud. And the Grahams, sitting across from her, were new ears for the old stories. No one else in their family had ever bothered to name a child after the first Winston on the continent. Whether it was true or not didn't matter. It was *their* family history.

"He and a group of men brought their families from Plymouth and settled in Boston."

And they were brutally attacked their first night. And ancestral Christopher vowed revenge. As usual the conversation had come around to the Winstons' long history in Boston. That meant the same stories hashed over and over. She liked that Christopher had a heritage she could attach herself to, but the poor Grahams.

She had known Christopher for three months, engaged for two of those months, and already she knew all there was to know about the Winstons. They liked to tell their glorious stories and assumed everyone liked hearing them. And they didn't always need fresh blood to tell them. She'd tolerate them ruminating about the past. . .at least for the next five months. Once she and Christopher were married on Valentine's Day, she could afford to tune them out. For now she'd be diplomatic and turned her attention back to her father-in-law-to-be.

"The savages kidnapped his wife and two daughters. And left his son for dead. When Christopher finally found their bodies, detestable things had been done to them."

Muriel Winston gasped but didn't detour her husband.

Rachel could never quite tell if Muriel's reaction was real or to embellish her husband's story. Lawton wasn't going into the horrid details this time, so Muriel's reaction was likely just for embellishment.

"Christopher nursed his son back to health, and the two of them rallied the men to take vengeance. Killed every last one of the savages. They had to make the place safe, after all."

Muriel closed her eyes for a moment and put her hand to her chest. Mrs. Graham was grimacing.

Rachel knew just how she felt. If the stories were upsetting, why keep telling them? If only there were some way to stop them.

Uncle Bert, sitting next to her, sipped his wine. "Why not tell the one about our cousin Palmer?"

Lawton Winston squinted his eyes at Bert. "Because I'm not through with Christopher's story."

Bert muttered something under his breath then said, "But Palmer is so much more entertaining."

Lawton deepened his glare. "As I was saying, all the Indians were killed, but so was his son."

Bert reached for the salt. "Excuse me, dear."

"Christopher married the daughter of one of—"

Rachel jumped from her seat with a gasp as her water goblet tipped into her lap. Clumsy Uncle Bert! Why didn't he ask her to pass him what he wanted? She swatted the water from her dress with her napkin.

Bert held out his napkin. "I'm so sorry, dear. Let me help you."

Christopher was at her side and shooing Uncle Bert away before she could tell him she could handle it on her own.

"I'll just go dry this off." She went to the bathroom and dried her dress the best she could. She couldn't even see where the liquid had been.

When she left the bathroom, she stared at the doorway to the dining room, then went to the library. She walked to the window and pulled back the heavy brocade curtain with the back of her hand. She just needed a little break.

"Sorry for the spill."

She spun around and saw Uncle Bert sitting in one of the winged chairs flanking the fireplace. "It was only water."

The firelight danced on his aging face. "I know. That's why I did it."

She widened her eyes. "You did that on purpose?"

He nodded. "I didn't think you were enjoying the story. . . again. You are simply too polite to leave on your own. And the Grahams certainly weren't enjoying it."

"No one likes that story." Rachel shuddered. "Why do they keep telling it?"

"They like to keep telling themselves that they are right and better than others. Justified in their grudges."

His frankness always took her off guard. She could never say anything so brash and still be a future member of this family. "Well, the stories are important to them. People shouldn't forget their heritage and what their ancestors had to overcome."

"History according to the Winstons?"

Was he implying that all the stories were fabrications?

"A lot of it is embellishment."

Embellishments? Not lies. "Don't most people stretch the truth a little?"

"A little?" He raised his graying bushy eyebrows. "It is hard to believe that every single generation had all heroes in the family. I did a little research on our family's founding fathers. I believe the area Christopher and the boys tried to settle all those years ago was a bit west of here."

"Really."

He nodded and leaned a little closer. "And I have an old journal that the family denies ever existed, which alludes to Christopher having kidnapped his second wife and that he went crazy. So don't believe everything they tell you exactly as it is told."

She never believed everything people told her anyway. People always had a hidden agenda. "Thank you for the advice—and the reprieve."

"Any time."

She smiled. "I should get back before *my* Christopher comes looking for me."

"Things broke up after you left. Everyone went to the conservatory to listen to Muriel play the piano."

"Everyone?"

He gave her a slight nod. "Everyone that matters. And in this family, I don't always matter, so they are all secretly relieved when I am absent."

Maybe that was because he wasn't afraid to tell the truth about the family's history. Or was it merely the truth according to Uncle Bert?

"I only attend my sister-in-law's little get-togethers to stir things up a bit. I wonder what a few generations down the road will say about the rebel in the family. What small thing did I do that they will twist and blow up to legendary proportions? I once saved a cat from a tree. That could make quite a story in a hundred years or so. Maybe it will turn out I really wrestled a tiger and saved a whole school yard full of children?"

"There you are."

Rachel straightened her shoulders as she turned to Christopher entering the room. She hadn't realized she'd relaxed her posture around Uncle Bert.

"Mother is playing Chopin."

She took Christopher's arm and gave Uncle Bert a slight tip of her head.

Bert held up his glass. "Enjoy."

Well, at least with her mother-in-law-to-be playing piano, the worn-out stories would cease.

❧

Three days later, Rachel reached for her umbrella in the entry closet. The express envelope slid to the floor. She took it to her black lacquer secretary and retrieved a sterling silver letter opener with a mother-of-pearl handle. It had been a gift from Christopher after she had suffered a paper cut while sliding her finger under the flap of an envelope. Christopher had scolded her, not for using her finger but for marring her perfect hands. She rubbed her index finger. No scar.

She slid the opener along the envelope's top edge and pulled out the letter. The letterhead identified Jacobson and Son as a law firm in Mackinaw City, Michigan. Why in the world would an unfamiliar law office be sending her anything?

She quickly scanned down the single sheet. According to these lawyers, she had just been bequeathed an inheritance from a relative she never knew existed. They must have the wrong person. She didn't know any Charles Dubois. But could it be she had finally found a connection to her past? Where there was one relative, there were others. Giddiness welled up inside her.

two

The horse-drawn carriage came to a stop in front of a white, single-level house with red trim on Mackinac Island. Rachel, wearing a cashmere coat over her silk pantsuit, wrapped her gloved hand around the metal bar as she climbed down out of the carriage. Crisp October leaves swirled on the ground where she stepped. "Could I get a hand with my suitcases?"

The driver shook his graying head. "Sorry, miss. I can't leave the horses."

She resisted the urge to bite her lip. It had been a long day, and all she wanted to do was get inside and take off her heels. This was evidently a self-service type of community. She went to the back of the horse drawn taxi and reached for one of her bags.

"I'll get that for you."

She looked into the brownest eyes she'd ever seen and stayed there a moment.

"Is this the only one?"

She pulled back her focus to a man with black hair tied back into a ponytail at the nape of his neck. "Those other two that match."

He hoisted her bags and set them on the ground, then walked to the front of the carriage. "I have all her bags, Duane. Thanks." He patted the side of the carriage. The driver flicked the reins. The clomping of the hooves mingled with the jingle of the harnesses as the carriage rolled away. The man with the incredible brown eyes picked up her luggage.

"I really appreciate your help."

"That's what neighbors are for." When he smiled, his eyes nearly squinted shut, a contented smile.

Maybe one day she would achieve that, too. After she was married. . . *Neighbor? He is a neighbor?* "You live close?"

He inclined his head to the house across the street. "The blue one. I'm Will Tobin."

"Rachel Coe. Pleased to meet you." She would have extended a handshake if both of his hands hadn't been occupied.

He stopped by her front door. "You have your key?"

Opening the screen door, she fished the key the attorney had given her out of her purse and was about to hand it to him when she realized that not only were his hands full with her belongings no less, but he was not Christopher, expecting to unlock her door for her. She swung the door open and stepped aside for him.

"After you." He nodded toward the door.

She stepped into the rustic-style living room and felt a warmth envelop her. This little house was quaint. She and Christopher could use it as a summer home. . .to get away.

"The lawyer called me and told me you were coming, so I came over earlier and made sure the water and electricity were on. I turned up the heat so it would be warm enough in here. It seems to be working."

"Thank you for going to so much trouble. You are very thoughtful. Did you know my grandfather, Charles Dubois?" It still seemed strange to call someone *grandfather*.

He hesitated a moment as though trying to decipher her question then nodded. "We were good friends. I spent time over here when I could."

She wondered about the wide, beaded choker around his neck. Unusual design. "You can just set those right there." She pointed to where he stood then pulled off her right tan leather glove and ran her hand along the top of a smooth log and branch table by the front door.

"Your grandfather made that."

A craftsman. "It's nice." A gallery of small photos adorned the wall behind it.

"He made all the furniture from fallen trees right here on the island."

She glanced around. All the pieces were the same log and branch construction. The tones were warm and comforting. "They're nice." So different from her contemporary black lacquer furnishing at her apartment. But she would need to replace it all; Christopher wouldn't like this style. Something art deco. Or maybe retro forties. Christopher might like that.

She ran her hand over an end table next to the couch. She would keep a few pieces in the spare bedroom. Christopher wouldn't mind that.

She took off her beret and shook free her dark, mid-shoulder-length hair, swinging it back over her shoulder. She didn't like wearing a hat, but it had been necessary on the windy ferry ride from Mackinaw City to the island. Time to thank her neighbor once again and send him on his way.

When she turned, the words froze on her tongue. Will stood staring at her with his mouth slightly ajar. It was a challenge not to smile. She loved that reaction from people, and it always took her by surprise. But it gave her a sense of worth even if it was only for her looks. *If you don't have your looks, you don't have anything.*

She held out her hand. "Thank you again for assisting me."

He shook it. "Uh-huh." He snapped his jaw shut. "Sure. No problem. I'm glad to help." He took a step back—right into the table by the door. "Oops." He turned to steady a small lamp on it that hadn't even been disturbed. "Sorry about that."

She had to smile then. She reached out for the door, but he reached faster and grabbed the knob. "I'll get that." He opened the door, but it stopped with a jerk against his boot. He looked down. "Big feet." He chuckled.

He managed to maneuver around the door and push open the screen door. He backed out and onto the porch. "If you need anything, just give me a call. I'm number five on the speed dial." He continued to get closer to the porch steps.

She point toward his feet. "Watch out for the steps."

As he looked down, his right foot slipped off the top step, and he stumbled down the rest.

She sucked in a breath.

He spun around but didn't fall and held up his hands. "I'm all right. I'm okay." He continued to walk backward toward the gate. "I'm fine."

She couldn't bear to watch what might happen, so she gave a little wave and closed the door then rushed to the window to peek out the edge where he couldn't see her. If he did injure himself, she wanted to be able to help.

He trotted to the gate, put one hand on the post then kicked his legs up and over the fence. She breathed a sigh of relief. He stood a moment looking at her house before he headed down the street—not toward the house he said was his, but another destination.

He was sweet and nice. It would be good to have him as a neighbor. Maybe he and Christopher would become friends.

Unbuttoning her coat, she turned back to the room. Where to put it? There was no entry closet to hang it in. There was no entry, period, to speak of. Once inside the door you just sort of fell into the living room. No barriers. No proving your worth before being granted admittance. Welcomed from the start.

Was she home at last? Had she found a place to belong?

A coat rack made out of a polished branch stood next to the entry table. Wouldn't that give Christopher fits. They could buy an armoire to replace the table. She hung her coat next to a leather one with beadwork and some fringe. She ran her hand down it. Her grandfather's? Why couldn't she have known about her grandfather before he died? There was so much she would like to have asked him.

❧

Will flopped onto Garth and Lori's couch. "Do you believe in love at first sight?"

Garth and Lori looked at each other, sharing a smile, and Lori giggled. Garth turned back to him. "I think after the way we met, it's safe to say yes."

"Then I'm in love."

Lori sat in an overstuffed chair crocheting an afghan. "Who's the lucky lady?"

"Rachel Coe."

"And who might she be?"

"Dancing Turtle's granddaughter."

"So she made it safely." Lori stilled her hands and set her project in her lap.

"I carried in her luggage. She has some similar features to Dancing Turtle. I could have picked her out of a crowd."

"Is she pretty?" Lori asked.

"Gorgeous."

She rolled her eyes.

"What? Is there something wrong with her being beautiful?"

"No. It's fine." She picked up her crocheting and focused on it.

He leaned forward, resting his forearms on his knees. "Tell me. I want to know."

Lori looked at Garth, who shrugged, then back to him. "I don't want to poke my nose in where it's not invited."

"I'm inviting you. Tell me what you think."

She set her work back in her lap. "It's just so typically male. You see a pretty face and suddenly you are in love."

"That's not true."

"How long did you spend with her?"

"Only a few minutes."

"So how can you know you are in love with her?"

He struggled for words to explain it. There had been something there from that first moment. A connection when their eyes met. He had sensed that she had felt it, too. A bond that went beyond either of them. "There was a connection between us that had nothing to do with physical attraction."

"There is more to Rachel Coe than what you see on the outside. She is a whole person with both good and bad to deal with. Look beyond her face and discover who she is. Love goes way beyond the skin."

"I concede. Maybe I'm not actually in love with her—yet. But it is the road I want to go down. The road I'm going to go down."

Lori put her work in the basket next to her chair and stood. "In that case you should welcome her properly with a gift."

"What? Like flowers?"

"I don't think your relationship is to the flower stage yet." She walked to the kitchen.

He looked at Garth who shrugged. "I don't know what she has in mind, but it's probably good."

He and Garth both rose from the couch and went to the kitchen. Lori was digging around in the cupboard. She pulled out a box of crackers, two cans of soup—one tomato, the other, chicken noodle—a can of peaches, and a jar of salsa. "Honey, can you grab a couple of plastic grocery bags?"

"Sure." Garth pulled two out from the lower cupboard nearest him.

Will watched, waiting for Lori to explain what she was up to. Curiosity got the better of him. "If you don't mind me asking, what are you doing?"

"I'm making you a 'Welcome to the Neighborhood' offering." She grabbed a bag of tortilla chips off the top of the refrigerator and a couple of apples from the basket on the counter. She began putting everything into the bags. "If she is going to be staying, she'll need food. Won't it be thoughtful of you to provide her with some so she doesn't have to find the store and buy something before she gets a little settled."

He smiled and stood up straight. "How thoughtful of me."

"Exactly." She pulled out a carton of eggs from the fridge and opened it. "There are five eggs in here. She can have those. I have another dozen in here." She handed them to him to put in the bag then came back with a loaf of bread and a stick of butter. "That should help until she can get to the store."

He gazed at the bounty Lori had provided him. "Lori, you're the best. Thanks."

Garth put his arm around his wife. "I think so."

She smiled. "Now go sweep her off her feet."

Will gathered the bags in one hand and headed off to Dancing Turtle's—or rather Rachel's. That would take some getting used to, but he was up to the challenge. He knocked on the door and waited. He raised his hand to knock again when she opened the door.

Rachel's mouth stretched into a smile. "You're back. Did you forget something?"

He held up the bags. "I brought food. Anything left here can't be any good."

She pushed open the screen. "That was very thoughtful of you."

He walked in and straight back to the kitchen, setting the bags on the counter. He pulled the items out of the bag and named each one as he did. "That should tide you over until tomorrow."

"You really didn't have to do this."

He ducked his head then looked her in the eyes, beautiful hazel eyes. Eyes he looked forward to getting lost in. "I must confess that it wasn't my idea. Lori gathered all this from her cupboards and told me you could use it. But I thought it was a great idea."

"Is Lori your girlfriend?"

"What?" How had she come to that conclusion? He didn't want Rachel to think he was attached in any way. "No. She's married to my friend Garth. I was just telling them you were here. I'm sure they'll come over and introduce themselves soon."

"That will be nice." She walked back to the front door and held it open for him. "Thank you again for bringing me food. I'll be sure to thank Lori as well. . .when I meet her."

She wanted him to go. That was obvious. He walked slowly to the door. She was probably tired from her trip. "I can come by after work tomorrow and show you where the store is."

"I might go exploring in the morning, and if it's not too far away, I'll probably find it. But thanks for the offer."

He stepped outside. "If you need anything, I'm—"

"Speed-dial five." She smiled at him. "I'll be fine."

He drank in her smile for a moment then left.

ea

Rachel watched Will leave again. This time he went through the gate in the conventional way. He had seemed reluctant to leave. She didn't want to be rude, but she needed to call Christopher and take a short nap before tackling the job of inventorying everything that needed to be done. There would be a lot, even for this little three-bedroom home. She would need to sort through closets and drawers and cupboards and completely clean out the entire house. Then decide which furniture to keep in the spare bedroom. It was all beautifully constructed. Would someone on the island want to buy it? Or better yet, she could give it to a charity. Yes, a charity, in her grandfather's name.

She would start in the main bedroom—no, the kitchen. She should do that right now. Get rid of any food that might be lingering.

The first cupboard had a dozen or so cans of canned food.

These should be fine. She pushed them around to see what was there. She pulled a couple out to throw away that she knew she wouldn't ever eat—canned ravioli and spaghetti. The next cupboard had some old crackers and a bag of unopened potato chips. She occasionally rewarded herself with baked chips, so those would go along with the crackers. The other cupboards either had dishes or other nonfood items like a phone book and papers.

The last cupboard had a handful of over-the-counter medications. She took them all out and found some bags under the sink and deposited everything she'd removed into them. There hadn't been much to get rid of. Either her grandfather didn't have much in the way of food, or someone had already cleaned things out. Will perhaps? She hoped if someone had been in here to clean that they hadn't overlooked the refrigerator.

She took a deep breath and held it before pulling open the door. The light came on, and the shelves were empty and seemed to have been wiped clean. The door held a few condiments and a jar of sweet pickles. She added it all to one of her trash bags. She put her two apples, eggs, and stick of butter on the shelf. She got a clean dishcloth out of a drawer and wiped out all the cupboards before putting the food Will had brought away and then wiped down the rest of the kitchen. She boiled a couple of eggs for a late dinner then found some clean sheets in a dresser drawer and remade the bed.

She climbed into bed and snuggled down into the covers. She felt as though her grandfather were giving her a hug. Tomorrow she would do some more cleaning, but she most wanted to find out if she had any other relatives living here.

Her eyes drifted closed, then she jerked them open. Christopher. She had completely forgotten to call him. She would do it first thing in the morning. It was too late now.

He was an hour ahead of her. What would he say about this place? Would he like it? He had to like it. Now that she'd found her family, she wasn't about to give any part of it up. She had to keep this house.

three

The next morning, Rachel padded to the kitchen. She could sure use a nice hot latte. Her gaze stopped on the cupboard above the stove. She had missed that one last night. Could it possibly hold something to make a hot drink? Yes. A box of hot chocolate packets and two old, battered tins. She pulled them down and took off the lids. They both appeared to have fresh, loose tea in them. One smelled fruity, like blueberries. The other was definitely mint.

She filled a teakettle with water and turned on the stove. So her grandfather made his own teas. She found a tea steeper ball and soon had a steaming cup of mint tea.

In the bedroom she leafed through the shirts hanging in the closet. She hadn't brought anything appropriate to do serious cleaning and sorting, so she chose a green and blue flannel shirt and wrapped it around herself. It was as though her grandfather were giving her another hug. If only she'd met him. She found a pair of drawstring sweatpants in one of the drawers and curled up on the couch, sipping her tea. She would call Christopher when she was done.

She walked over to the front window and pulled open the curtains to greet the new day. The sun was creeping up the horizon. Her gaze settled on the blue house across the street. A blond man in a heavy coat on a bicycle pulled up front and waited. Soon Will came around his house pushing a bike. Was this the island's form of a carpool?

The attorney had said there were no cars on Mackinac Island. They obviously took that seriously. Will turned to her house. Could she duck out of the way? Will smiled and waved. Too late, he'd seen her. She waved back. The two men rode away.

Time to get to work. She would spend the first few hours surveying the house and getting acquainted with her grandfather. Then she'd walk to town or wherever to the nearest store. This wasn't that big of an island. A store couldn't be that far away.

She had taken a quick peek in each of the other two bedrooms last night, one a bedroom, the other used as an office-type workroom. She went into the bedroom first. A quilt made out of pink floral patterns donned the bed. Whose room had this been? Her mother's? She sat on the bed and rubbed her hands over the quilt. *Why did we never come back here, Mom? Were we even ever here?*

No clothes hung in the closet, but it was piled high with boxes. What was in them? Not one was labeled. She made a mental note of things to sort through. The dresser drawers were full of linens, memorabilia, papers. . .and junk. The bed had boxes stuffed under it, and a couple more stacks of boxes occupied the corner. This room would take a while.

The office was more of the same—stuff to sort, most of which she would pitch. She was drawn to a small loom on a table near the window. Beadwork, similar to what Will had been wearing around his neck yesterday, decorated taut strings on the loom. She stroked the beads. What kind were they? She had never seen any like them before. The leather coat out on the coat tree had these same kinds of beads. Very unique.

A divided dish on the table held beads of various sizes and shapes. There were also some finished pieces on the table—a beaded bag and a beaded band the size of her wrist, similar to the one Will wore. With a little effort, she managed to attach the band around her wrist.

A knock at her door startled her. Who would be visiting her at this hour? She looked at her watch. After ten already?

She hadn't realized how long she'd lingered. She hurried to the door and opened it.

A woman with red hair stood on her porch. "Hi. I'm Lori Kessel, one of your neighbors. I wanted to welcome you to the neighborhood."

She pushed open the screen door. "I'm Rachel Coe. Would you like to come in?"

"Thank you." Lori stepped inside.

"Are you the one who gave Will the food for me?"

Lori grimaced slightly. "He was supposed to take credit for that, but yes."

"I thanked him, and I'd like to thank you as well. That was very sweet of both of you."

"I remember what it was like when I moved not all that long ago, to want a little something to satisfy a nagging hunger without having to go out."

"It was very nice to have something on hand, but I can't live on what you and Will provided forever. At some point I'll have to venture out. Is there a store around here?"

Lori gave her directions and explained that people often went to the mainland, where things were cheaper, to do the bulk of their shopping. They talked for a while longer; then Lori said, "I can't think of a better place in the world to live than right here on this island. You are going to love it here."

"I already do." At least what she'd seen so far. She would have to talk Christopher into coming often. She would help him fall in love with the place, too.

Lori left shortly after that.

A little while later, she walked the neighborhood and found the store, where she bought a few things.

It was dinnertime before she remembered she still hadn't called Christopher. She dug her cell phone out of her purse and noticed her bare ring finger. Where had she left her ring? She found it on the bedside nightstand where she'd left it last night. She slipped it on and dialed Christopher. Nothing was happening with her phone. *No service.* She walked toward the living room window and got one signal-strength *boop*—then no service.

She shook her head. She would have to use the conventional phone. Hopefully it was in service. The attorney had said that all the utilities were on. Did that include the phone? She glanced out the window before turning away but quickly turned back.

A girl about eight, bundled in a coat, stood outside her gate staring up at the house. Her black hair was braided like an Indian's.

Rachel opened her front door and stepped out into the cold. "Hello. I'm Rachel."

The girl just stared.

"Did you want something?"

"To see."

To see what?

She rubbed her arms as she watched the girl slowly walk away. *That was weird.*

Rachel went back inside and to the phone in the kitchen. She lifted the handset but the spiral cord was twisted around itself, so she leaned down. *Yes, a dial tone.* She worked to untangle the cord then placed a collect call.

"Baby, I've been so worried about you. I've called your cell phone several times and left messages. Why didn't you call last night?"

She didn't dare admit she hadn't called because she hadn't thought about him much since arriving on the island. "I'm sorry. I've just been so busy here, I lost track of time. And then my cell phone doesn't work here."

"I'm just glad you're safe. Is the place nice?"

"It's a cozy little cottage."

"Is it in good repair? Will we be able to sell it quickly on the market?"

Her stomach twisted. "I don't want to sell it, Christopher. You should see this island. It's a resort island, and they only have horses here, no cars."

"Baby, you know I'm not fond of horses."

"You don't have to ride a horse. There are horse-drawn carriage taxis that will take you anywhere you want to go. Or you don't have to do that at all. The people here ride bicycles to work. This would just be like a summer getaway place."

"You sound excited about the place—more excited than you are about selecting our wedding invitations."

How could invitations compare to Mackinac Island? "Just give this place a chance. If you really hate it here, we can talk about selling it later." But she wouldn't, she couldn't. Christopher simply had to be given the opportunity to fall in love with the place, too.

"If you really want to keep it that badly, we'll give it a go."

Why did that concession make her feel as though Christopher was slipping away from her? "I'm already making plans to refurnish the place. It has this really great rustic furniture my grandfather made. . .but it's not really our style." *Or rather not his style.*

"Whatever you want to do with the place is fine with me, baby."

Which meant he was placating her until after the wedding; then he'd try to convince her to sell. Well, when his father had the prenuptial agreement drawn up, she'd be sure to include her being the sole owner this house. She would not let it be sold from her. It was her link to her past. She would make Christopher see that keeping the house was the best thing to do.

That night she dreamed about Indians attacking her home and trying to take it away from her. The girl with the braids watched from the side.

❧

The next day, bundled in her coat, Rachel headed for the

library to do a little family research. The librarian told her the best person to talk to would be the high-school history teacher. The K-12 school wasn't far, just up the road, but she was hardly dressed for hiking around town, and the taxi that had dropped her off was long gone. She pulled on her gloves and marched out. It wasn't far. She could make it in her heels.

Once at the school office, she asked for the high-school history teacher.

"He should still be at lunch. I'll send for him." The secretary gave a slip of paper to a student who left.

"Thank you."

"Excuse me." The secretary turned to answer the phone, so Rachel turned to a bulletin board and perused the announcements there.

"Rachel!"

She spun around. "Will? I didn't know you worked here."

"High-school history and English. Kally said a beautiful woman was asking for me in the office."

She widened her eyes. "You're the history teacher?" Had she known, she might not have come. There was something about Will Tobin that drew her in. Whatever it was, she couldn't let it happen. She was engaged and wouldn't entertain thoughts of anyone else. She would keep anything between them strictly business.

"I'm the one you want."

"You are?" No, Christopher was the one she wanted. She straightened out her thoughts. "I was at the library, and the librarian sent me over here."

"How can I help you?"

"I was just wondering if I had any other relatives on the island."

"Dancing Turtle was collecting information on every family member he could to create a family tree."

"Who?"

"He had a brother who, I think, had three children—"

She waved her hands in the air. "Who is this Dancing Turtle?"

"Your grandfather, Dancing Turtle."

Her insides twisted, and she dared not to breathe for a moment. "That sounds Indian."

"We prefer Native American. Columbus thought he'd reached India."

"My grandfather was Ind—Native American?"

"Ojibwa. So am I. A lot of the islanders have some Ojibwa or Ottawa blood in them."

She stared at him stunned. Yes. It was there. His long hair; the wide, beaded choker; the structure of his face. Will seemed to drift into the distance. If her grandfather had Indian blood in him, then that meant she—Oh, Christopher. His family detested her sort. What would they say about having one in the family? She knew exactly what. They would not tolerate it for one moment, as they hadn't tolerated a cousin for having a Korean wife, even though she was sweeter than all them combined.

"Thank you." She turned to leave. She needed to get back. Needed time to think and sort this out.

"Rachel." A hand on her arm stopped her, and Will came into focus. "Are you all right?"

"I'm fine."

He released her arm. "I'll come over after work and help you find that information in your grandfather's things."

It didn't matter. She just needed to get alone and think. "That's fine. Whatever works for you." She walked out the door but stopped suddenly when she noticed a girl just outside the door staring at her—the same girl who had been at her house last night.

She hurried down the cement path to the street. When she

got back to the library, she called a taxi and waited outside for it to arrive.

Dancing Turtle? Ojibwa? How could she be part Indian— or rather Native American? There had to be some mistake. The taxi came and took her home. She stood outside the gate and stared up at the house. The house she'd come to love already. She took a deep breath of the crisp fall air and went up to the door and inside. Her breath caught. It wasn't rustic, it was Indian. It was so obvious. How could she have not seen it before? The gallery of framed photos of Indians. Were any of them Charles Dubois? And the black-and-white drawing of a man turning into an eagle. Or was it an eagle turning into a man? One thing was for sure, the man was Indian.

She sat in the chair adjacent to the couch then immediately shot out of it and spun around. Was this furniture of Indian craftsmanship? What did it matter? She sat back down and rubbed the beaded bracelet her grandfather—Dancing Turtle—had made then put her hands to her face.

Everything she'd worked so hard to achieve was suddenly slipping away. She wished she'd never come.

❧

Late in the afternoon, Will walked up to Rachel's door with chicken parts to fry, rolls, and a Caesar salad in a bag. He knocked and waited. He knocked again. He peeked in the front window through a gap in the drapes. The place was dark and seemed deserted. Where could she be? He took the groceries back to his house and called her. No answer.

Was she all right? She had been a little pale when he'd seen her earlier today.

He wrote a note for her to call him when she got home, including his phone number written out. Just in case. He stuck it to her door and left.

four

The next day Rachel unlocked the door to her Boston apartment. The harsh black furniture slapped her in the face. Nothing warm and inviting here.

The taxi driver set her suitcases inside the door. She paid him and closed the door. The apartment seemed stuffy, and even though it was cold outside, she opened some windows. She unpacked her suitcase and threw in a load of laundry before calling Christopher.

"Baby, you're back."

How did he know that?

"My heart jumped for joy when I saw your apartment number come up on the caller ID."

That's right. She didn't have caller ID so never thought about other people having it even when she knew they did.

"When did you get in? It doesn't matter. I'm just glad you're back."

How could she tell him who she really was? Or who she thought she might be?

"I'm coming right over," he said.

"As much as I'd love to see you, too, I'm really tired. It's been a long day. I'm going to turn in as soon as I hang up."

"I could come and stay with you."

She heard the hopefulness in his voice. He had been getting more and more persistent about starting the honeymoon long before the wedding. Her mother had told her to hold out for the ring. She gazed at the engagement ring on her hand. This one? Or the wedding band? She never said. "We agreed to wait until after the wedding. It's not that far away. Only four months."

He didn't say anything for a moment. "I'll take the morning off and come take you to breakfast then."

"I'm going to have to pass on breakfast. I have an early call in the morning; then I'm heading right back to Mackinac Island." She wouldn't have come back if it weren't for the one-day modeling job she'd agreed to weeks ago. She'd almost forgotten about it.

"What? So soon? Why do you have to go back at all?"

"There is a lot to do. There is a lot of junk to get rid of." She had to purge the house of anything Indian related before Christopher ever saw it.

"We can hire someone to do that."

"I want to do it. A hired person wouldn't know if there was something of my grandfather's that I would want to keep." It may not be the most desirable heritage, but it was hers, and she wanted to hold onto at least a little of it.

"What about planning our wedding? You have a lot to do there, as well."

"I can do that, too." Besides, her mother-in-law-to-be had all the connections and was doing most of the planning. Muriel would show her five different wedding invitations, and she'd just have to pick one; three different place settings, and she'd pick one. Should the reception be here or there? Muriel had great taste and often agreed with Rachel's choices. Her wedding was going to be bigger than anything she had ever imagined—five hundred guests. Most of whom she wouldn't know. The only thing Rachel absolutely had to be around for was choosing and fitting her one-of-a-kind designer wedding dress. There was plenty of time for that. "I want us to be able to stay at my grandfather's house on Mackinac Island for a few days at the end of our honeymoon." If she still had one.

"I don't think that will work out. I've almost planned the whole honeymoon." He chuckled. "But I'm not going to tell you where. It's a surprise. You'll love it though. I promise."

She hoped she got a chance to love it. But still she felt Christopher slipping away from her. When she knew something for sure and not just hearsay, she'd tell him.

"I'll drive you to the airport. What time do you leave?"

That was a compromise they both could live with.

ஐ

Late Sunday night, she stepped back into her house on Mackinac Island and filled her lungs with fresh air, exhaled, then inhaled deeply again. She could breathe again. What was it about the air here that made it so cleansing?

Soon someone knocked on her door. "Will?"

"I saw the lights on. I was worried when you didn't answer your door or phone on Friday night."

She hadn't wanted to face anyone after the news he had given her earlier that day and had ignored the world. She had needed to sort things out. She still did. Going back for the job hadn't afforded her any time to think.

She had locked the house and taken the next ferry off the island. She'd stayed that night at a hotel near the airport in Alpena, but she knew ignoring it would not change anything. She had decided on the second leg of her flight that she had to come back and find out if it was all true. So before leaving the Boston airport she had booked her returning flight.

"Is everything okay?"

"I had to rush back to Boston for work. But I'm back for a while to sort through things." Not just the things in the house but things in her head, as well. "I'd still like to hear about any relatives I might have, but right now I'm really tired."

"I can come over after work tomorrow."

She forced a smile. "That would be great."

Tomorrow she would find out the truth. And what her future might hold.

She changed into some flannel pajamas that had been her grandfather's and curled up in the bed. She stared at the framed artwork on the wall in the moonlight of an Indian maiden with a wolf at her side. The maiden looked exotic and proud. As the moonlight shifted, the picture crept into the shadows, but she could still see the maiden in her mind.

What would she do if she were indeed part Ojibwa? Would she be proud of her ancestry? Or deny it? She had always wanted an ancestry, a heritage. But did she want it badly enough to risk her future with Christopher? She could share his legacy.

❧

Late the next afternoon, there was a knock on Rachel's door. Her insides flipped. That would be Will. She would finally have her answers. She opened the door.

"I hope this is a good time." He held up a bag. "I brought dinner. Mind if I take over your kitchen for a while to make it?"

She stepped aside for him. "Go right ahead." A man cooking for her? She couldn't pass that up.

He headed for her kitchen and called back over his shoulder, "I hope you like spaghetti."

She used to, but she didn't usually eat pasta anymore.

After pulling out a pan, he unwrapped some ground meat from white butcher paper and dumped it in. He pulled a jar of store-bought spaghetti sauce from his bag. "My secret ingredient." He set a pan of water on to boil. Precut, prebuttered French bread and salad from a bag rounded out his meal.

Her stomach rumbled softly at the aroma of the cooking meat. She drank it in. How long had it been since she had beef?

When everything was ready, he pulled two plates from the cupboard and handed her one. "You go first."

She scooped a few noodles onto her plate and a spoonful of sauce and took some salad. She skipped the bread and went to sit at the table.

He joined her with a full plate. "You don't eat much, do you?"

"I'm really not hungry, but I wanted to try some." Her stomach was still in knots over what she might learn tonight, despite its small rumble earlier.

"Shall I bless the meal?"

Pray? Why not? "Sure." She bowed her head as he did and then raised it after he said amen.

He twisted spaghetti onto his fork. "I'm glad you're back. I was worried. Not knowing what had happened I just kept praying for you that everything was okay."

That was sweet of him, but she didn't like it when people said they were praying for her. She felt as if she owed them something in return. They prayed for her, and so she would be expected to do something for them.

"Did my grandfather have any other children besides my mother?"

"Not that I'm aware of."

That was disappointing. She had hoped.

"But he did have a brother. That's where you'll find your relatives."

"Do you know any of them?"

"I met one of them once. There was some kind of break between Dancing Turtle and his brother. He never talked about it. I could tell it pained him."

"So I do have relatives living on the island?"

He hesitated. "Yes."

"But—"

"None of them would talk to or acknowledge Dancing Turtle. He was, like, removed from the family. If they won't acknowledge him, they may not you, either. I don't want you to be disappointed."

She might have family, and they were going to be stubborn? She turned her mind to another issue that interested her.

"How did my grandfather come by the name Dancing Turtle when his legal name is Charles?"

Will smiled. At a memory she assumed. "Your grandfather was never in a hurry. So he was called Turtle. I could walk back and forth to town twice before he ever got to town. He took his time in everything he did."

She rubbed the beaded bracelet around her wrist. "Even his beadwork."

He touched the choker at his throat. "He waited for the piece to speak to him and tell him what it wanted to be."

"Did he make yours?"

He nodded. "He said it would help me find my way."

"And did it?"

"I have no clue. I never understood what he meant by it, and he wouldn't tell me. I don't feel lost at all."

"So where did the Dancing part come from?"

"At the Ojibwa-Ottawa ceremonies, he participated in the tribal dances. The only time the Turtle would move very fast."

"Do you have an Indian name?"

"Native American. And yes."

Native American. She had to remember that. "What is it?"

"If you're done, we can go to Dancing Turtle's office and see about that information you wanted." He picked up their plates and walked to the kitchen.

She followed him. "You are avoiding my question. If you don't want to tell me, then say so."

He put the plates in the sink. "Squandering Arrow."

She had to smile at that. "How?"

"I don't exactly hit what I'm aiming for when we go hunting." He walked to the office workroom.

"And you squander the arrows."

He sat at the desk with the computer and turned it on. "It's not as easy as it looks, and I am improving. The last time out I shot a deer. That was ground venison in the sauce. Okay.

I only wounded it, and Dancing Turtle had to take it the rest of the way down."

"Do all Native Americans have a—a Native American name?"

"A lot do, but not all."

"What would mine be?"

"I don't know. I'd have to know you better. A name isn't given to you. It is who you are. Boys are often named after weather, stars, or animals, and girls after flowers, bodies of water, or times of day." He turned back to the computer when it completed the boot cycle. "I put a program on here for Dancing Turtle to build his family tree. Let's see if he ever used it." He scrolled through file names. There weren't many. "It looks like he hadn't gotten around to it yet." He sighed. "I guess we have to do this the old-fashioned way."

"And what way is that?"

He waved a hand toward a stack of boxes in the corner. "Hard copy. Hopefully he'd gotten around to gathering it all in one box to put into the computer. But if I know Dancing Turtle, he didn't."

She gazed at the tower of boxes. This wasn't going to be as easy as she thought.

"I really have no business going through what are now your things. Do you want me to help you?"

"I'm not ready to tackle all this tonight. Can you give me a brief overview of what you know about my grandfather's family, so I'll kind of know what to look for?"

"I don't know very many details, just general stuff." He motioned toward the door. "Let's go sit in the living room."

Rachel nestled into the chair and tucked one leg under her. "Anything you can tell me will be great."

Will sat on the couch. "From what I understand, your grandfather has been collecting information for years and stuffing it away in boxes. He wouldn't talk much about his family but would tell me that he found more information on your grandmother's family ancestors or another birth certificate or ship's manifest. He was like a giddy child with a new bit of information."

"So whom do you know about?"

"Dancing Turtle has a brother named Lewis Dubois, tribal name Twin Bear."

"What does that mean?"

"Either that he has two sides to him or that half of him is lost and he's incomplete, but either way the bear is a sign of strength, and you don't want to make him angry."

"You said that I would have relatives on his side. Did he have children?"

"Two or three. He has a daughter named Emily. I don't remember her married name. I met her once. She might live on the island. I'm not sure about the others."

"For being my grandfather's friend you sure don't know much."

He raised one shoulder and let it drop. "Dancing Turtle was a very private man about his family. He once alluded to there being a dispute over your mother being his daughter or not. He insisted she was, said he had proof."

That was an interesting bit of news. If she weren't blood related to Charles Dubois, then Christopher's family would have no problem with her. But if she wasn't Dancing Turtle's granddaughter, then whose was she?

five

Late the next afternoon, Rachel stood and stretched from digging through one of her grandfather's boxes in the office, and made herself a cup of tea. So much to sort through. She wanted to go through it all at once: the office, the master bedroom, and the spare room. So much to learn in so little time.

She wandered into the living room and stopped in front of the wall of a dozen or so small, framed pictures, all of Native Americans, some in regular clothes, others in costume. Were they all Ojibwa? Were any of them related to her? Were any of them her grandfather? She longed to have known him, longed to have had the chance to ask him so many things.

Her gaze settled on a three-by-five sepia-toned photo of a young woman about seventeen or eighteen, posed to look over her shoulder. It appeared to be a school photo, with no distinguishable background. She would guess from the hairstyle and age of the photo that it was taken in maybe the forties.

She set her cup on the entry table and lifted the wood-framed photograph off the wall. What caught her most was the resemblance to herself, her oval face, the lift of her cheeks, the shape of her eyes. Were they hazel like her own? There may be a question as to whether or not she was related to Charles Dubois, but somehow, someway this woman's blood flowed through her veins. Was this her grandmother? The slight smile on the young woman's face seemed to say yes. A tear slipped down her cheek. *I wish I had known you.*

A knock at the door pulled her out of her thoughts. She

swiped the tear from her face with her fingers, then looked down at her grubby work clothes. No one who knew the Winstons would be here, knocking on her door. She saw no need to concern herself about her appearance. She opened the door. Her neighbor Lori stood on her porch with a handsome blond-haired man that must be her husband. He held a basket in his hands.

She swung the door wider. "Come in."

Once inside, Lori introduced Garth. Lori pointed to the basket as Garth handed it to Rachel. "This is to welcome you to the neighborhood."

"Thank you." Rachel set it on her coffee table. The basket held a couple of books, a candle, two apples, an orange, and a box of tea. That would come in handy. She was running low on her grandfather's blends. She pulled out the tea. "Can I make you both a cup of tea?"

After she had brought them their steaming mugs, they all sat in her living room.

"Did you know my grandfather?"

"Sadly, no," Lori said. "We moved in the week after he passed away. I'm so sorry for your loss."

She was sorry, too. "I never met him either, but I wished I'd had the chance."

Later that evening, after an early dinner, Rachel stood at the front window with a mug of steaming blueberry tea cupped in her hands. She just loved her grandfather's teas. The fruity scent filled her nose. She blew some steam away and took a small sip. Still too hot to drink.

A lone headlight came up the street. It wasn't a motorcycle because it didn't make any noise and was too slow. Soon she saw Will, bundled and chugging in the dark on his bike. He must have worked late. She left the window and went back to the kitchen. She slipped off her engagement ring and laid it on the counter before washing up the few dishes she'd dirtied for dinner. She set the last dish on the towel to dry when a knock sounded on her door. Grabbing another towel, she dried her hands on her way to the door.

"Will, I wasn't expecting you. Come in out of the cold."

He stepped inside. "I thought you might need some help going through those boxes. Maybe a name will jump out at me, or I'll remember something I didn't know I knew."

"That would be great." Anything that would help her discover her heritage. She closed the door. "I saw you coming up the street earlier. You looked cold out there."

He took off his coat. "I wish it would hurry up and snow."

"Wouldn't that make it harder and colder?"

He shook his head. "Much easier. Then I can pull out my snowmobile and cruise back and forth to work. This time of year is hard when it's cold but hasn't snowed yet. Even worse is spring when the snow is all slush and neither snowmobile nor bicycle are any good."

"There are no cars on the island, but you can drive snowmobiles? Doesn't that defeat the purpose of having a no-motorized-vehicle rule?"

"When cars were first being brought to the island, the carriage drivers petitioned to ban cars because they scared the horses. When snowmobiles came out, residents pressured the park commission to allow their use on the island. Finally, they bowed to the local pressure and granted snowmobile use on one road leading from Harrisonville to the ice bridge. Since then, a few more roads have been opened up to snowmobile travel, but most of the island is still off-limits to snowmobiles."

"Interesting. By the way, your friends, Lori and Garth, came by earlier. They brought me a welcome basket." She pointed to the basket on her coffee table.

"They're great people."

"Lori invited me over for tea tomorrow."

"I don't know her well, mostly through my friendship with Garth. The way he talks, she is an angel. You should get to know her."

Was that hope in his voice? Why should it matter whom she became friends with? Or if she became friends with anyone?

Will held out his hands from his sides. "So what can I do to help?"

She tossed the towel on the kitchen counter and led him to the office where they sat on the floor across a box from each other and began digging. "I started pulling things out of boxes and making piles." She had spent most of her day riffling through box after box searching for her mother's birth certificate or something else, anything else that might have Charles Dubois's name associated with her mother's. Nothing.

"What have you found so far?"

"I'm not sure. Maybe nothing. Maybe everything. I don't know what any of it means."

He surveyed the mess she'd made across the floor. "What's in all the piles?"

She shrugged. "Just stuff I pulled out. I was looking for my mom's birth certificate or something else that told who my parents were. You said that there was a debate as to whether or not Charles Dubois was indeed my grandfather."

"Well, I can tell you that you are definitely related to Dancing Turtle. Besides that, it is obvious you are Ojibwa."

That brought a smile to her face, but it shouldn't have. She could lose everything she had worked for because of it. She wanted to be someone's granddaughter, but what about Christopher? If she was indeed Charles Dubois's granddaughter, she could lose Christopher, but if she wasn't related to Charles, then she would be back to having no family of her own.

"Why don't we start with you sorting one box, and I'll sort another."

After sorting for an hour, mostly reading, she stretched her back. "I'm running out of space." She looked around her. "Each piece of paper seems to need a separate pile."

Will looked over. "What are they all?"

"I think these have to do with my grandfather's family. . . maybe. Those belong to my grandmother—I think. And the rest—most of them—I haven't a clue."

"Why don't you gather up all the ones for your grandma in one pile and put them aside? And do the same for the undetermined. That will make more room for the others."

She hated to do that. She wanted to see all the information at once. But it did make sense. She pictured her grandmother's face as she began stacking her piles and an ache filled her. *I won't forget you.*

six

Will took a deep breath before knocking on Rachel's door two nights later. He hoped she would be as inviting as the last time. He just wasn't sure what to think of her. He was getting mixed signals. He sensed she wanted him as a friend, but there was something more. He was sure there was. There was for him. He was completely taken by her. It was Friday, and he could stay a little later. Hopefully.

The door opened and Rachel smiled. "Will. I'm so glad you are here."

His heart melted again at the sight of her, and he could feel his mouth spread into a wide lazy smile as he stepped inside. Her excitement warmed him. He could feel them drawing emotionally closer. He held up a plastic grocery bag. "I brought steaks, rice, and fresh broccoli."

"That was sweet of you, but I don't usually eat beef."

That was disappointing. His smile sank. "It's not beef. It's venison." Maybe that would make a difference.

"From the deer you wounded?"

Don't remind me. He nodded.

"Well, your venison was good in the spaghetti, so I guess I can give the steak a try, but first let me show you what I've been doing. I had this revelation last night, and I want to know what you think."

"It looks like all those boxes exploded." Paper lay on every available horizontal surface.

She waved a dismissive hand. "I just couldn't stand to have it all stacked up. When I came across a name I had read before, I couldn't find it again. So now they are more or less alphabetical. The *A*s start in that corner. But what I want to show you is in here." She headed for the office room.

He quickly put the bag of food on the kitchen counter and followed the narrow path of uncluttered floor. Once inside the room, she motioned toward a mostly bare wall.

He stared at it for a moment. The art was gone. He wasn't sure what to think. "You are taping white paper over a white wall? It really doesn't change the look of the room much. And I'm not seeing it as the next hot decorating trend."

"It's not decoration. I'm going to cover the whole wall with paper. Then I'm going to pin these at the top of the wall." She handed him three small beanbag animals, one a turtle, the other two were small brown bears. "I'm going to build my grandfather's family tree under the turtle and his brother's under the bears. I found them in the spare bedroom. I wonder if my grandfather had them because of his and his brother's Native American names?" She walked up closer to the wall and spread her hands above her head as though she were smoothing the paper. "I'm going to pin up birth certificates, marriage certificates, newspaper clippings, anything he collected on the family. I'm going to build the family piece by piece."

"That sounds like. . .an interesting way to organize it. Then we can put it into a database on the computer." He had always been curious about Dancing Turtle's finds, but the old man wouldn't share. He would find a new bit of information and hold onto it like a child with a piece of candy, saying when he got everything and put it in order, he would let Will have access to the information.

Will was somewhat of an expert on the Native American history of the island but hadn't traced any specific family. His ancestors, way back when, used to come to Mackinac generation after generation, but when the British and French and new Americans took over the island, his ancestors didn't return with the other tribes. They mixed and mingled with the people on the mainland. Why couldn't his family have returned like the others? Then maybe his blood wouldn't be so blemished with undesirable sorts.

"I'm not great with computers. Can you show me how to put the information into the computer?"

"I can do that part for you." If he showed her, then she wouldn't need him as much. But if she insisted, she would still need him to help her. "That way you can focus on organizing all the information." His feeling's for her grew stronger each time he was with her. He sensed she felt it, too. He wanted to reach out and just touch her.

"Okay." She turned away from his gaze. "Shall we get dinner going? I'm starved."

Was she a little shy? He followed her to the kitchen and soon had the white rice cooking and the seasoned meat on a broiling pan in the oven.

She cut up the broccoli and put it in the top of the steamer pan. "A man who can cook. That's impressive."

"Well, don't be too impressed. I can only cook about three things and just substitute a different meat for variety. I like my meat well done. How do you like yours?"

"Well done."

"Something in common." He liked that. He opened the oven door and surveyed his masterpieces inside. "I use premixed herbs and spices on everything." He handed her a bottle of garlic and herb mix. "The only thing I have in my spices collection. It's on the steaks, and I put some in the rice. We can put some on the broccoli, if you want."

She smiled at his gusto for his little mixture, but it really went with everything and made cooking at least semidoable. "Let's try the broccoli plain. It will add variety to the already *seasoned* food."

He nodded and leaned one hip against the counter and

watched her graceful movements as she continued to chop the broccoli. "So, you don't eat beef, and I assume you don't eat bread because you didn't have any the other night when I brought dinner. You also don't seem to eat spaghetti, because I know it wasn't the spaghetti because it was perfect." He usually burned the noodles to the bottom of the pan, and the sauce came from a jar. "You hardly took any. So what do you eat?"

"Don't get me wrong. The spaghetti was great. I just don't indulge in too many carbs."

That explained it. He would have to remember that. "Do you eat rice? Or will I be eating all that myself?"

"I usually only eat wild rice, but I want to try some of your *seasoned* rice."

That sounded like a diplomatic answer. "What do you indulge in?"

"Chicken, fish, and vegetables, steamed, stir-fried, fresh. There is a lot you can do with vegetables and such a wide variety. I'll have to cook for you sometime." She put the steamer of broccoli on the top of the pan of boiling water.

His mouth pulled up on one side. "I accept." She must feel their connection, too, and wanted to spend more time with him as he did her.

While they waited for the food to finish cooking, she took two plates from the cupboard and silverware from the drawer and set them on the counter. "My head is swimming with all the information I have gone through so far. I can't keep any of it straight. That is why I came up with the idea of pinning it all to the wall, but some of the people I have come across, I have no clue where they will fit on the tree. Honestly, I have no idea how I'm related to most of these people."

"I know Dancing Turtle has been collecting information for years, so finding and organizing everything might take you awhile. Maybe if you just started out making piles, like all the birth certificates or all the things that mention Dancing

Turtle and a pile for the people you have no idea how they connect, then you can pin up the people you do know and hopefully start filling in the unknown people."

"It sounds like a great big jigsaw puzzle of a picture that is shades of all one color, and I don't even have all the pieces."

He smiled. Was she inviting him to spend more time with her? "I like puzzles."

Rachel poked a fork in the broccoli. "I think these are done. Shouldn't you check on the meat?"

He jumped away from the counter and pulled open the oven door. A small plume of smoke wafted from the opening. The edges of the meat were black. "I hope you like yours well-*well* done."

❧

Rachel savored her last bite of venison. The edges may have been singed, but the rest was divine.

Will picked up their plates and headed for the sink. "Sorry about burning dinner. That's usually how I eat—blackened and charred."

"It was still tasty. I think it must have been your special blend of spices."

He turned from the sink with a grin.

Good. She hated to see people grumpy. They returned to the office, and she stared at the open boxes on the floor. "My head is still spinning from my last dive into those boxes. I've spent most of the day pulling stuff out and reading it only to discover I have no clue what it means. If it means anything at all."

She was afraid this huge task was going to take more time than she had. She had to be back in Boston in a week. She wanted to have this all sorted out and filed away in an orderly fashion so Christopher wouldn't see any of it. And she wanted to find out for sure if Charles Dubois was her grandfather. If not, then she didn't have to worry about telling Christopher she was part Native American because she wouldn't be.

"I think I'm going to just hang paper on the wall for now. My eyes are still a little tired from earlier." Rachel lined up another sheet of white printer paper on the wall and leaned her shoulder against it as she reached for the scotch tape in her back pocket. It wasn't there. She hadn't put it back in her pocket. She glanced over her shoulder to the desk and saw the tape next to the stack of paper on the corner. She splayed her hand out over the paper on the wall and reached for the tape. It was just out of reach.

Will grabbed it. "I can help with that." He studied her a moment before pulling off a piece then pressed it on the seam between the two sheets of paper.

She moved her hand before her fingers got taped to the wall as well.

When she had put up the last sheet, she turned from the freshly papered wall. Will was right there, inches from her, pressing something onto the wall next to her.

"This one was coming loose." His eyes locked on her, holding her in place. Neither spoke. He seemed to be studying her face, her mouth.

Surely he wasn't thinking about kissing her? No, he couldn't. He began to lean toward her.

She turned and stepped away from him. This was really awkward, and she didn't know what to say. She heard him draw in a deep breath behind her.

"I should get going."

"Okay." That was a relief. "Thank you for all your help." She walked to the front door.

"I can't come back tomorrow. I promised to fix some things around my mom's house on the mainland, but my Sunday afternoon is free."

How did she tell him he probably shouldn't come back? Or had she misinterpreted his actions, and he never intended to kiss her at all? Christopher always said she was a little naïve when it came to reading men.

Will continued, "Speaking of Sunday, would you like to go to church with me?"

"I'm not into religious rituals." And it might be best to keep some distance from him.

He stared at her as though he couldn't believe what he'd heard. "You don't go to church?"

"No."

"Never?"

"I went a few times when I was a child, but it never really did anything for me."

&

Religious rituals? Never did anything for her? Will sat on the edge of the brown leather recliner in his living room. *Lord, how can someone be in Your house and not be moved by Your Spirit? Unless their heart is hardened. How could I have fallen for someone who is not a Christian?* Good thing he hadn't kissed her. *Lord, that had to be Your hand. Thank You for keeping me from making that mistake. But what do I do now? I like her. I like her a lot.*

He stood and paced the room. *Do I just forget about her? I don't know if that is possible.*

He wished Garth was around to talk to, but he and Lori had gone to visit his parents for the weekend. He wouldn't be able to talk to Garth until Monday at school. He heaved a heavy sigh and headed off to bed.

seven

Will leaned into Garth's classroom just before the first bell rang on Monday morning. Garth was taking off his coat. His friend had made it on time. When he had called to find out where Garth was this morning, Lori told Will that Garth had overslept and had just jumped into the shower. She urged him to go on to school alone.

He patted the door frame. "Glad to see you made it."

Garth ran a hand through his blond hair. "Barely."

"That's all that counts. Are you busy for lunch?"

Garth shook his head. "What's up?"

"I just need some advice." The bell rang, and he patted the frame again. "I'll meet you in here." He stepped across the hall to his room.

When the lunch bell rang and the hallway had cleared, he grabbed his lunch and rolled his desk chair to Garth's room. Garth was still talking with a student. When the student left, Will blessed their food.

Garth picked up half his sandwich in one hand and a pen in the other. "What's up?"

Will peered over to see what Garth was working on. "You didn't get your papers graded over the weekend?"

"Only my last period class. They won't take long, all multiple choice. I'll have them done in no time."

"If you're busy, I don't want to interrupt you."

"I can grade these and listen at the same time. What's bugging you?" He took a bite of his sandwich.

Will reached into his lunch sack and was about to pull out his sandwich when a boy walked in.

"Mr. Kessel?"

Garth looked up. "Hi, Shane. What can I do for you?"

"I need some extra help with math." Shane was a senior with a mild learning disability that made learning in the traditional ways challenging for him at times, but he tried hard and for that Will had often given him the benefit of the doubt when grading his papers and tests.

Will stood and grabbed the back of his chair. "I'll catch you later."

"Come over for dinner tonight. We can talk then."

"Will that be okay with Lori?"

"Sure."

❧

Will and Garth still sat at the table after dinner. Lori had gotten up and was in the kitchen. "I invited Rachel to church."

"Great. How'd it go?"

"It didn't. She's not a Christian." He knew that meant any romantic relationship he hoped to have with her needed to be put on hold.

"What are you going to do?"

"I've prayed, but I'm not sure. And forgetting about her isn't going to work because I tried that all weekend. What can I do? She didn't sound very open." And giving up on her wasn't an option.

"Do you feel you are supposed to try to lead her to the Lord?"

"I think so. I've been spending time over at her place helping her sort through Dancing Turtle's things. Maybe I can work on her, tell her about the Lord and all the wonderful things He has done in my life. Talk about how great our church is and hopefully make her curious enough to want to go. You don't think that will be too obvious and pushy?"

Garth shrugged. "It's hard to tell. It depends on how

hungry her heart is for spiritual truths. People are sometimes searching and don't even know it is God they are seeking."

"The one thing I won't do is try to kiss her again. . .for now. It would only confuse things."

Lori set a plate of chocolate chip cookies on the table harder than normal. The cookies jumped a little. "You tried to kiss her?"

He looked up at her staring down at him. "I was seriously thinking about it, but the moment passed. What's so wrong with that? I know she's not a Christian, but I'm still attracted to her. And maybe a friendship between us will help bring her to the Lord."

Garth took a cookie. "But, Will, don't expect her to come to the Lord just to please you."

He knew it needed to be real and personal for her. "I know, but it would open that door, and church is just the place to start if I can figure out how to get her there."

Lori held up her hands to form a *T*. "Time out, boys."

Will grabbed a cookie from the plate, as well. "You don't think it is a good idea for me to win her over for the Lord?"

"I think it is a great idea." Her lips curved up in a sad sort of smile.

"But. . . ?" He could tell Lori had more to say. A lot more.

She took a deep breath. "Haven't either one of you noticed the rock the size of this island on her left ring finger?"

"What?"

"I'm sorry, Will, but she's engaged."

He dropped his cookie onto the table. "That can't be."

Lori shook her head slightly. "Unless she wears a large diamond ring on her left ring finger for fun, she's spoken for."

❧

Rachel peeked out the front window. Will stood on her porch, facing her door. She couldn't very well ignore him. He knew she was home. She had done a lot of thinking and decided it would be best to play things safe and tell him not to come around just in case. She had enjoyed his company and help, but she couldn't let him think it was leading anywhere. She opened the door.

"Can I come in a minute?"

She hesitated.

"Only for one minute." He looked like a lost puppy.

She opened the door wider. He stepped inside, and she closed the door.

"I just want to know one thing." He grabbed her left hand and stared at it. "Are you toying with me?"

She yanked her hand from his. "What are you talking about?"

"Lori says you have a significant engagement ring. I've never seen you wear it."

She stared at her outstretched hand. Where had she left it this time? She was always worried about damaging it. "I took it off when I was doing dishes. You interrupted me. I forgot to put it back on." She walked to the sink and came back with it. "See." She slipped it on her finger.

He raked his hands through his hair, loosening it from his ponytail, then walked in a tight circle in place. "I didn't know. I promise you I didn't know."

That was a relief. She didn't like thinking of Will as a man who would knowingly move in on another man's woman.

"I never would have tried to kiss you the other night if I had known."

"I appreciate you telling me that."

"Why didn't you tell me you were engaged?"

Was he accusing her of being deceptive? "It wasn't any secret. I wear my ring all the time." She had taken it off a lot lately with all the cleaning she was doing but never purposely to hide her engagement from him. It was coincidence that he'd never seen it.

He sighed. "But you could have told me."

He was accusing her. "I find it a little awkward to introduce myself, 'Hi, I'm Rachel Coe, and by the way, I'm engaged in case you were planning to have feelings for me. Because I think every guy I meet is going to fall for me.' Or maybe I should have just waved my engagement ring under your nose to show you how much my fiancé cares?"

"Instead you let me make a fool of myself by coming over all the time. I even made you dinner. Twice." His voice rose the more he spoke.

She gritted her teeth and tried to school her growing frustration. "I thought you were being neighborly."

"There's neighborly and then there is interested."

"And how am I supposed to tell them apart? How was I to know you never saw my ring? It's not like it is that discreet." Christopher had made sure of that.

He pulled his eyebrows way down. "I don't know. You just do."

She frowned as well. "Well, I didn't."

"Well, you should have."

She was tired of being yelled at. "I think you should leave now."

"I'm already gone." He walked out and slammed the door.

She stared at the door and took a deep breath. At least everything was out in the open now.

A small ache welled up inside her at their friendship being severed. She had to focus on Christopher. She still had him until she found out whether or not she was Ojibwa. Part of her desperately wanted to be Dancing Turtle's granddaughter. Even though he'd never met her, he cared enough about her to leave her everything he owned. But another part of her wanted to walk back to Christopher and leave all this trouble behind her.

&

Will climbed out of bed. His digital clock read 1:03 a.m. Sleep eluded him. He scrubbed his face with his hands and walked to his living room window. Pulling back the curtains, he looked across the street. Her house was dark. Why shouldn't it be in the middle of the night?

Lord, how could I have gotten so carried away? I thought she was that one special girl for me. The one You chose for me. How could I have been so wrong?

The connection he'd felt obviously wasn't real. Just wishful thinking. . .or his overactive imagination. The Lord would never direct him to someone already spoken for, and the Lord certainly wasn't the author of his feelings for someone who wasn't a Christian. Even so, his feelings for her were real enough, and they hadn't just poofed away with this new bit of knowledge. He wished they had.

At twenty-eight, he'd been content with his life, his job. He hadn't been looking for someone to spend the rest of his life with. Oh, he wanted to get married someday, but he didn't feel any rush to make it happen; let it come when the Lord chose. Then *bam*! Rachel happened, and his whole outlook on his future had suddenly been turned upside down and brought into focus. Now having a family of his own had suddenly become a priority. But not just any family—a family with Rachel. He shook his head. He couldn't have that and had to stop thinking about her.

He let the curtain fall back into place and walked back to bed.

He had to stay away from her. Somehow. That was all there was to it.

Except he'd handled it all so badly. He'd have to apologize.

The next day, Will motioned Garth from his classroom before the start of the next period. "I'm going to head over to Rachel's house."

"Do you think that's wise?"

He had his prep period just before lunch, so he should have plenty of time. "I'll be back by the end of lunch." And he didn't want to put it off.

"No. I mean about her being engaged."

"When I left your house last night, I went over to hers."

"I thought you probably did."

"I ended up yelling at her. I need to apologize. I shouldn't let any more time pass." Even though he knew he should stay clear of her, he also knew he owed her an apology.

"Is that the only reason?"

He kept telling himself it was.

&

Rachel studied the photographs on the wall. Was the woman she assumed was her grandmother in any of the other pictures? She couldn't find her in any of them. Was this the only picture? If the woman in the one photograph was her grandmother, shouldn't there be more? Pictured with other family members? It was almost as if her grandmother was a phantom or figment of her imagination. Why was there this one picture of her and no others?

She startled at a knock at the front door. Just after eleven. The only person this time of day she could imagine coming over would be Lori. She pulled open the door. Her smile dipped. "Christopher."

He smiled. "Surprise."

She glanced over her shoulder at the paper-strewn living room then down at her flannel shirt hanging out over her sweat pants. Her impulse was to close the door and make things right before inviting him in.

"Aren't you going to invite me in?"

Was there any way she could gracefully say no? "Of course. Come in." She closed the door behind him and began rushing around the room scooping up her carefully laid piles into one big messy wad. "Sorry about the mess. I told you there was a lot to go through."

He set his bag by the door. "Don't worry about that right now. I just want to look at you and hold you."

She dropped the papers into the chair and smoothed her hands down her flannel shirt. "I'm a mess. I'll just quickly go change."

He snagged her arm as she passed and pulled her into his arms. "I just want to hold you for a minute first." He kissed her.

Why did his show of affection make her feel uneasy? He was her fiancé after all. Shouldn't she want him to kiss her? Was it her conscience nudging her because she was keeping a secret from him? She stepped from his arms. "I'll just go put on something more suitable."

"I'll look around a little and get a feel for the place." His gaze scanned the room.

"I'll only be a minute." She'd better hurry. She didn't want him looking too closely. She shucked her work clothes and slipped on her silk pantsuit she'd been wearing the first day she arrived. She checked her appearance in the bureau mirror. Oh no. She'd forgotten she had parted her hair down the back and braided each side. She'd wanted to put herself in the mood of her ancestors as she sorted and it kept her hair out of her way. She yanked out the bands at the bottom of each braid and raked her fingers through her hair. She tried fluffing it with her hands but couldn't erase the memory of her previous look. Hopefully Christopher would quickly forget. She grabbed her ring off the nightstand and slipped in on then took a deep breath and pasted on a smile before stepping out of her bedroom.

Christopher was at the wall of pictures. Not just standing by the wall but destroying the wall. He removed a picture and stacked it with the other two he'd already taken down.

"What are you doing?" She didn't care that her voice had a sharp edge to it.

He smiled. "Just helping out. These can't stay." He turned around and pointed to the picture of the Native American turning into the eagle. "And that will have to go as well. I know you've been busy and just haven't gotten around to it yet, so I thought I'd give you a hand. The faster this gets done, the sooner I get to have you back in Boston."

She meticulously returned the photographs to the wall. She wasn't sure she wanted to be in Boston any longer—everyone worrying about status and the pressure to do and be perfect. The expectations. She had thought that was what she wanted, but now she wasn't so sure. She felt more herself here.

"I've been thinking." Christopher walked across the small living room. "It may be hard to sell a place like this in the winter, so we can keep it until after the honeymoon. I think we should leave the furniture and sell it with the place."

Christopher obviously hadn't been listening. He thought that by allowing her to keep this place until after the honeymoon that she'd be willing to sell it. She wouldn't sell. It could be a breaking point between them. If it weren't for her Ojibwa blood that would tear them apart. "I'm not selling it."

"I know not right away but eventually." He turned to her with a smile. "We can't keep it."

"Why not?"

"It's hardly big enough. There would be no place for a housekeeper for starters, not to mention any other staff. And if you did manage to wedge a housekeeper into that spare room, there would be absolutely no privacy for us." He came over with that consolatory look in his eyes and put his hands on her shoulders. "If your heart is set on this island, then we can buy a more appropriate house. I saw some lovely ones on the bluff from the ferry. Or we could rent a suite at the Grand Hotel for a month at a time. No worries, no hassles."

She didn't want another house or the Grand Hotel. She wanted this house, but was she willing to put her foot down now to keep it, or should she wait until after they were married? "Maybe we can keep it, too."

"Why keep it if we will never use it?"

She stepped from under his hands. "We might. You never know."

Before he could respond—and she knew he would—someone knocked. She whirled around and opened the door. Surprised, she blinked several times. "Will. What are you doing here this time of day? Shouldn't you be at the school?"

"I'll only be a moment. I couldn't let any more time pass before apologizing to you. I'm sorry for my behavior last night. It was uncalled for."

"It was a simple misunderstanding."

Christopher eased the door from her hand and opened it all the way. "Hello. I'm Christopher Winston, Rachel's fiancé." He wrapped one possessive arm around her waist and thrust the other out toward Will.

Will's mouth pushed up in a stiff smile, and Rachel wondered if Christopher could tell it wasn't real?

Will shook Christopher's outstretched hand. "Nice to meet you. I'm Will Tobin. I'm *your* neighbor across the street."

Had Will gritted his teeth when he said *your*? This had the potential to get ugly real fast. "Thank you for stopping by, Will." *Now please leave before someone says something I'll regret.*

Will gave her a quick nod. His forced smile seemed to soften when his gaze turned to her; then he left.

She took a deep breath as she closed the door and turned to Christopher.

Christopher was frowning. "What was that about?"

She headed for the kitchen. "Nothing really. Just a misunderstanding. You want some tea?"

"No, thank you." He followed her. "I don't like him. He doesn't have a trustworthy face."

How could he tell anything about Will from his face? Maybe his Native American heritage if he cared to notice. Or was it was the Native American look he didn't trust?

The whole incident had been embarrassing for her—and not due to Will. She looked at Christopher's scowl. How could she be embarrassed by her own fiancé? She busied her hands in making the tea while she explored her current feelings. How committed was she to Christopher in her heart, anyway?

ॐ

Will jammed his bike into the bike rack. He had thought he had given Rachel and the whole situation to God, but seeing her fiancé just boiled his blood. She was really taken, and he had to stay as far from her as he could get. . .living across the street from her. And do a lot of praying.

He went to his classroom. His prep period wasn't even over yet. He put his face in his hands and stayed that way until long after the lunch bell rang. When he heard his door open and close, he raised his head.

Garth pulled up a student chair next to his desk. "Did you see her?"

He nodded.

"Didn't go so well?"

He raised his lips in a sardonic smile. "Went great. Until I met her fiancé."

"Ouch. Was he a jerk?"

"Not really. He's probably a great guy, and she will be happily married for the rest of her life."

"While you are lonely and miserable?" Garth's eyebrows rose up in question.

"Yup." He leaned back in his chair. "How do I get her off my mind? Just praying hasn't budged her from my thoughts one iota."

"There is no better cure to dissolve infatuation than to start seeing someone else."

That sounded like a terrible idea. He didn't want to see anyone else. "Have you ever tried that?"

Garth nodded.

"Did it work?"

Garth hemmed and hawed. "Not exactly."

"You are recommending something that doesn't even work?"

"That's because I was meant to be with Lori."

He rolled his eyes. "So what makes you think it will work for me?"

"You obviously aren't meant to be with Rachel."

"I think that is the problem. I haven't accepted that yet. So how do I accept it?"

"Lots of prayer."

He didn't mind spending more time in prayer, drawing closer to the Lord; it was the ache inside that bothered him most. He just couldn't help how he felt about her.

eight

Christopher pointed to his suitcase near the front door. "I'll just leave this here for now."

She wanted to say no, but she bit back the word. It didn't matter. He wouldn't be staying. He wouldn't want to. He had grown up hating her and didn't even know it. Though she hadn't found the proof yet, just Will's word, in her heart she knew she was part Ojibwa. How long could she avoid telling him? He deserved to know. Now or later, what difference did it make? The result would be the same. Her fairy-tale life would come to an end.

She took her tea into the living room and sat on the couch. "Come sit with me. I have something I need to tell you."

He sat next to her. "Is this about that Will Tobin guy? I knew I didn't like him from the minute I saw him."

She put her hand on his arm. "No, this has nothing to do with him. It has to do with my grandfather—who my grandfather was." Her stomach knotted.

His shoulders relaxed. "What is it?" He frowned. "Don't bite your lip."

She released it.

He took her hand. "You always do that when you're nervous. There is nothing to be nervous about. It's just me."

Yes, just you—who hates who I am. She knew she had to tell him. It wouldn't be right to keep this from him. Her lineage shouldn't matter, but it did to him and his family. "I'm Ojibwa."

"You're what?" He took his hand from hers.

She wouldn't lie to him. "I'm probably at least one quarter

Ojibwa. The Ojibwa lived on this island many years ago."

"You're an Indian?" He stood.

She stood, too. "Native American."

"You can't be."

"But I am. Maybe your parents won't mind." It was empty hope.

He jerked around to look at her. "They'll mind all right. I can't believe this. Did you know about this before?"

"No."

"Well, this ruins everything." He thought for a moment. "Wait. We can fix this."

"What?"

He put his hands on her upper arms. "Grease the right hands, change a few documents, and you have a whole new history. After all you hardly look Indian. Mother and Father never have to know."

Will had commented on how much she did look Ojibwa, not just Native American, but like her specific people. "Native American," she ventured to say, not that Christopher would ever care to use the politically correct term. Maybe some people, people like Christopher's family, preferred the term *Indian* because it made the people who were here first seem like the foreigners rather than those who came after them.

"The point is you don't have to be *native* anything. We can create the right kind of heritage for you."

Right kind? It seemed as though Christopher had inherited his family's ability to make up their own version of history. "Changing who I am on paper would somehow take the Ojibwa out of my blood?" She finally had a lineage, a heritage. And he wanted to take it away from her.

"No one knows. And no one has to know."

"I'll know. You'll know."

"It'll be perfect. I promise." He took her in his arms. "I love you."

When he leaned in to kiss her, she pushed away from him. "No, you don't. You love what you think you can make of me—the idea of who you want me to be."

"Baby, let's be reasonable about this."

"And you consider bribing people, falsifying documents, and lying to your family reasonable?"

"I love you, baby. I want this to work. I can make this work for us."

She shook her head. "You can make it work for you, but not *us.* Not me. I want to be Ojibwa."

He stepped back from her, hurt on his face. "Baby, I did everything for you. I taught you how to dress, what to say, even how to furnish your apartment. But I didn't do all that for my benefit." He put his hand to his chest. "You can wear whatever you want for me. I did it so you could fit in easily with my family. So they could find no fault with you. I love you. I wanted you to be accepted unconditionally."

"But there were conditions, Christopher. If I dressed, behaved, and did everything as I should, then I would be accepted. I don't want to live like that. I want to be me."

"Then be yourself."

She felt certain he was trying to convince her with false words—words he thought she wanted to hear.

"Ojibwa? Your family wouldn't let up on you until you were rid of me. They would make life miserable for both of us."

"Then we'll cut ourselves off from my family."

She shook her head. "You could never do that."

"I could."

No, he couldn't. He depended on their approval. He needed it as much as the air he breathed. She, on the other hand, depended only on herself. She had thought she wanted social status, but this is what she really wanted. A background, a heritage, even if it was less than perfect. But then who had an ancestry that was? Christopher could no more leave his family and heritage than she could leave hers, and she would prove it to him. "We could elope today, and you could move in here with me? In this tiny house?"

His eyes widened. "What about mother? She would have fits. I could never do that to her."

Exactly. He wanted to keep her, but his instincts always went back to his family. What else had he told her because it was what he thought she wanted to hear?

His features slacked. "I would be disinherited."

She just stared, feeling sorry for him.

He raked a hand through his blond hair. "Why are you doing this? I thought you wanted a home and family?"

She had both here. "I'm Ojibwa, Native American, Indian. Your family can't live with that. And now that I've discovered it, I can't live without it. This is who I am. And your family will hate me for it. You will come to hate me for it, too."

She had never been as committed to Christopher as he was to her. It was his status that drew her to him—a status she once thought so important. Now it seemed so frivolous. So his leaving wouldn't really be a loss. She could live without the status and without Christopher. Christopher had known that she didn't love him the way he said he loved her, but he wanted to marry her anyway. What he really wanted was a trophy, and she had wanted to please and to fit in his family. But love? She had assumed that would come in time. Christopher had convinced her it would.

nine

After she came back from her November photo shoot, Rachel knocked on Will's front door. He had been avoiding her. And for good reason. He still thought she was engaged. She was here to bring him some good news. . .and invite him to dinner. Two weeks in New York had been good for her.

She pulled her coat tighter around herself. Low snow clouds hung in the sky. She could feel the coming snow in the air even though it hadn't started falling yet. It would soon. When Will opened the door, she smiled brightly. Will did not return her cheery greeting. No matter. "Can I come in? It's cold out here."

The muscle in his jaw flexed as though he were clenching his teeth, but he opened the door wider for her to enter. He closed the door behind her but stayed beside it and didn't offer to take her coat.

She pulled at the fingers of her gloves as she scanned the living room. Brown leather furniture, thick heavy tables, wrought iron lamps. It wouldn't take Sherlock Holmes to deduce this was a bachelor pad. "You have a nice place here."

"What can I do for you?" His words were cold.

She turned to face him as she draped both gloves in her right hand. "It's what I can do for you."

He raised one disbelieving eyebrow.

She continued before he could protest. "I promised you a home-cooked meal, and I intend to make good on that promise."

His mouth pulled into a thin smile. "I think it's best if I decline considering the circumstances."

He'd already proved that he didn't always take note of a woman's left hand, so she would make sure he did this time. She held out her left hand to him. "Circumstances have changed."

He studied her bare hand for a moment. "I hope that had nothing to do with me."

She shook her head. "Christopher's family had a little problem with me being Ojibwa."

He pulled his brow down. "Why should that matter?"

Exactly. But it did. She waved her hand in dismissal. "It's a long story. And believe me rather boring. So does seven work for you?"

"I still don't know if it's a good idea."

"Why?"

He rubbed the back of his neck, and his pained expression said he was trying to find the words to say what he wanted to say as kindly as possible.

The stunned look he had given her when she had said she didn't attend church flashed before her. Was he that prejudiced that he couldn't even have dinner with someone who didn't believe as he did? "Is this because I don't hold the same religious beliefs as you?"

"Well, there is that, too."

"Too? So you want nothing to do with me because I'm not religious like you. Christopher doesn't want me because I'm part Native American. My stepfathers didn't want me because I wasn't theirs. Can't anyone accept me just as I am? Do I always have to change and be someone else to please others?"

"It's not like that."

She moved toward the door, but Will was standing in her way. "Let me go."

"Please let me explain. I don't want to be some rebound romance to get you through your pain and then tossed aside."

She leveled her gaze at him. "Who said anything about romance?"

"Isn't that what this is about?" He lifted her left hand. "Why you showed me your vacant finger?"

She yanked her hand away and clenched her teeth. "Please let me leave."

"I'm sorry. Can we sit down and talk about this?"

"I don't want to talk. I want to leave." She pulled open the door as far as she could and pushed herself out. She needed to escape.

She stopped in the middle of the street and took a deep, calming breath. Snow had begun to drift out of the sky. She caught a flake on her bare hand. Each one beautiful. Each one different. Why couldn't people be accepted the same way? It melted, and she shoved her hands into her coat pockets.

She had gone over in such a good mood and look what he'd done to it.

⊷

Will watched Rachel until she was inside her house; then he picked up the phone. It rang and rang and rang. Maybe it was too soon for her to talk to him. Should he go over to her house? He shook his head. She would probably just ignore his knocks as well.

He'd made a mess of things tonight. He should have just said, "Sure I'd love to come to dinner." The news of her breakup was still unreal. He had been trying hard to get his mind on other things besides her. . .without much luck. He didn't want to be a stopgap between this fiancé and the next.

He knelt down in front of his recliner. He hadn't knelt to pray since he was a child, but it seemed so right. There was power on his knees. *Lord, wrap your loving arms around Rachel tonight. Help me know how to help her.*

He'd been praying more than usual since trying to get Rachel out of his head, and the Lord kept impressing one thing on his heart—*be her friend.* He'd told the Lord that there was no way, at this point, that he could just be her friend. He couldn't be around her and her fiancé, soon-to-be husband, and not be bitter or angry or want more than friendship from her. Maybe this was what the Lord had in mind. He knew she would be breaking up with her fiancé and would need a friend, and the Lord wanted to prepare him for that. *Okay, Lord, I'll be her friend. . .if she still even wants me as a friend.*

⊱

Rachel had successfully avoided Will for the rest of the week, and then he left. Probably to see family for Thanksgiving. He'd said his mother lived on the mainland. After Thanksgiving, she avoided him again for a few days, but the day before she was to leave for the Caribbean for another photo shoot, she found a present on her doorstep in a black gift bag with colorful stars on it and bright blue tissue paper sprouting from the top. He must have left it on his way to work this morning. She would march right over to his house and return it to him, except he wasn't home yet. It would have to wait until he got home for her to tell him no thank you.

The bag sat on her coffee table the rest of the day. Every time she glanced at it, which was often, it seemed to whisper *open me.* The sooner Will came home, the better.

As the afternoon slipped away, she sat on the couch staring out the front window, waiting for Will. She wasn't even going to wait for him to take off his coat. She wanted the gift gone. She glanced at it.

Open me.

It was in a bag after all. Will would never know if she peeked inside. She lifted it onto her lap. It was heavy for the size. What had he given her?

She pulled out the tissue, then a book. *The Holy Bible?* Just when she was beginning to think he was sweet for thinking of her. All he wanted to do was change her. She opened it to the presentation page. *To Rachel Coe, from Jesus Christ.*

Was that some kind of joke? Will didn't even have the nerve to sign his own name?

She sucked in a quick breath at the sound of the phone ringing. She set the Bible aside and answered it.

She recognized the voice of Mark from the modeling agency she worked for. "How would you like to go to Europe?"

Europe? She had always wanted to go to Europe. "What is this all about?"

"I have been invited on a special European photo shoot in January, and I can bring any model of my choice. I want you."

"But we already have a January photo shoot there in Boston." She stretched the cord into the living room so she could see out the front window. Will should be home any minute now.

"We can move that if you still want to do it, or Ryan and one of the other models can work it."

"I don't know. I was planning on taking some time off." How had Mark gotten her number anyway? Probably from Christopher. She didn't want to contract any more work right at the moment until she sorted out her personal life.

"This is Europe, Rach. I've got to have you. You're the best. You have the look I want to shoot over there."

If that look was Native American, then she definitely had it.

Will drove up the street on his snowmobile. "Can I think about it?"

"I've got to know soon to make the arrangements. I'll see you the day after tomorrow in the Caribbean. I'll convince you on that shoot that Europe will be the right choice."

She walked back to the phone base on the wall. "Fine. I'll see you there. Bye."

She shoved the Bible and tissue paper back into the bag and swung on her coat. He'd had plenty of time to park his snowmobile and get inside. She knocked. When Will opened the door, she held out the bag. "I can't accept this."

He slipped his hands into his pants pockets. "Does it say it's from me?"

"Well, no, but. . ."

He kept his expression neutral.

She couldn't read him. "Who else would have given it to me?"

"I don't know. What does the tag say?"

She gritted her teeth. "There is no tag." And he knew it. But she couldn't prove he was the culprit. "I know it is you. Just take it."

"I can't take something that isn't mine. I guess you'll have to keep it." He was infuriating. How could she get him to take it back? She probably couldn't.

She spun on her heels and went back to her house. He hadn't said he didn't give it to her, just that it wasn't his. Just because she still had it didn't mean she ever had to take it out again. She set the gift bag on the floor next to the entry table and hung her coat on the tree. She had packing to do if she was going to leave on the first ferry in the morning.

ten

Two and a half weeks later, Rachel rode in a horse-drawn sleigh toward her house. Mark had talked her into the Europe job, so to honor their Boston January job, Mark arranged for them to do that shoot on the heels of the Caribbean shoot. She was exhausted. She'd made him promise he wouldn't ask her to do any other jobs for at least three months. She knew taking time off was the right decision, regardless of whether or not it was a wise career move. She wanted to sort through the house and decide what she was going to do about everything. The house, Christopher, work, staying or not. And Will. She had thought about him a lot while she was gone. Wondering what he was doing, and if he ever gave her a second thought.

He'd been right not to jump into a relationship with her. She needed time to really get over whatever it was she'd had with Christopher. She had liked the security of knowing she'd have a family if only by marriage. Now she felt lost and alone.

The sleigh stopped in front of her house. She gazed at the little one-story structure. Home. It felt right to be here. Like a hug from the past. She stepped down. Snow crunched under her feet, and she hefted her suitcase off. "Thank you."

"Have a good day," the driver said, then snapped the reins.

As the sleigh jingled away, she looked at Will's house. He was likely still at work. It was probably best not to get involved with anyone at this point, and Will obviously thought her lack of religious beliefs was some sort of flaw in her. Well, she could do fine without him or anyone.

She noted that her walk had been shoveled. Will? He may not admit to anything, but she knew.

She opened her screen to unlock her door and an envelope fell out. She picked it up. Nothing was written on it. Once inside, she set down her suitcase and sighed. Home. She hung up her coat on the tree rack and took the envelope to the couch. With one leg tucked under her, she pulled out the flap and took out the single sheet of paper. It was a list of names and contact information. The first name listed was Lewis Dubois, her grandfather's brother. After his name was written, "lives with oldest daughter, Charlotte Smith (middle child), on mainland," then an address and phone number. Next was "Gray Dubois (eldest) also on mainland." The last name listed was Emily Newton with her full address and phone number—here on the island! Then at the bottom "Please don't be disappointed."

Will strikes again. Who else?

She waited until she heard his snowmobile drive up the street then waited another five minutes to give him a chance to get inside and take his coat off before picking up the phone. She pressed speed dial five.

Will seemed relieved to hear from her. "You're back. I didn't know if you had left for good or not."

"I had to go to the Caribbean for work."

"I thought you were from Boston."

"I am, but I travel a lot for my job."

"I never asked you what you did for a living," he said.

"I'm a model, but I'm going to take a hiatus and sort through my grandfather's things."

"I should have guessed you were a model. So are you going to be around for a while?"

"Through the first of the year, then I have one last job in January before all my commitments are done." She took a deep breath and bit her lower lip. "Are you going to be around?"

"Only until Friday. Saturday I'll head off the island and visit family over the holidays. What about you? You aren't going to be alone are you?"

Yes, she would. She had no family to spend it with, here or anywhere else. She looked at the paper in her hand. Unless this family would welcome her. "Don't worry about me. I wanted to thank you for shoveling my snow and for the list. I'll see if any of my family is free."

"Rachel, please don't get your hopes up. I wasn't sure if I should give it to you because I'm afraid you'll be hurt."

"So why did you?"

"I figured you would eventually dig up the information as I did."

"How did you get all this?"

"I asked around and did a lot of digging. I eventually learned that Twin Bear's youngest daughter lives on the island and has two children here at the school, elementary- and middle-school age, so I'll eventually have them. I asked the older one about his family. I got enough info to look up the rest."

That was so nice of him to do all that work for her even after they'd fought before she left. "Thank you. I really appreciate it."

"Have you tried to contact anyone?"

"Not yet. I wanted to thank you first, in case I don't feel like it afterward."

"Just promise me you won't put too much hope into them accepting you."

Hope was all she had. "I'm a big girl. I think I can handle it."

After hanging up, she stared at the paper. Who to call first? She would start at the top and work her way down. She dialed Charlotte with excitement and trepidation, then bit her lower lip.

"Hello," a female voice came through the line.

She released her lip. "Hello, is Charlotte there?"

"This is she."

Her stomach flipped. "Hi, I'm Rachel Coe." The line went dead. "Hello? Hello?" Had Charlotte heard her? She redialed.

The phone rang and rang, but no one picked up.

Yes, Charlotte heard me.

She dialed the son. Maybe she would have better luck with him. No answer. Had Charlotte called to warn him? No. If she had, the line would likely be busy.

She dialed Emily. A child's voice came on the line. Was that the child who had been outside her house? Will said her children were young and went to the school. "May I speak with Emily Newton?"

The girl practically yelled into her ear. "Mom! Phone!"

She held the receiver away from her ear.

Soon a woman came on the line. "Hello?"

She took a deep breath. "Hello, my name is Rachel Coe." She waited but Emily said nothing. "Hello? Are you still there?"

"I shouldn't be talking to you."

"You know who I am?"

"We all do. I have to go."

"Wait, please."

"I'm sorry, but I really shouldn't talk to you. Please, don't call here again." *Click.*

She lowered her hand with the receiver in it. What should she do now? Call back? She said not to, so she probably wouldn't talk to her. Wouldn't anyone in this family at least talk to her?

The next afternoon she tried the son again. A young male voice came on the line.

"May I speak to Gray Dubois?"

"He's not available right now. May I take a message?" The words droned out of the teen as if they had been programmed in.

If she left her name, he would likely not call back.

"Hellooooo. Can I take a message?" the boy said.

"No. I'll call back later."

"Suit yourself."

"Wait. Why does your family hate me?" She cringed. She shouldn't have blurted the words out, but now that she had, she might get an answer.

"Do you want me to write that down word for word as a direct quote?"

Smart-alecky kid. "I would like an answer."

"It all depends on who you are. There could be a variety of reasons why my family hates you. So many people. So much hate. Personally you sound like you could be cute, so I don't hate you."

He may, after she told him who she was. "My name is. . . Rachel Coe—Please don't hang up on me."

"No way!"

"I called Charlotte Smith and Emily Newton."

"Don't bother with them. My aunts won't talk to you."

"Will you? Or are you going to hang up on me, too?"

"Man, you've made my day. My enemy's enemy is my friend."

"Excuse me?"

"I hate my dad, my dad hates his dad, and Grandpops hates you, so therefore you're my friend."

That was a bit backwards. "Why does everyone but you hate me?"

"Charlotte Coe."

The boy whose name she didn't know told her about brothers, Charles and Lewis, who were in love with the same woman. It tore the brothers apart. Charlotte couldn't stand to come between the brothers and left, pregnant with one of the brother's baby.

Mom.

"Grandpops never got over losing Charlotte even after he married Grandma. It broke her heart when he insisted on naming Aunt Charlotte after his old love. Aunt Charlotte bends over backwards to please the old coot. Dad thinks she is trying to make up for not being Charlotte's child."

"That is so sad."

"This whole family is one big mess."

"Would your grandfather see me?"

"Why in the world would you want to see him?"

"You are the only family I have."

"You're better off without."

She didn't think so. Wasn't even a dysfunctional family better than no family at all? "I'd like to try."

"You must be really hard up if you want anything to do with this family."

"I just want to know my family."

He heaved a sigh and was silent for a minute. "We are all meeting this Sunday at Aunt Charlotte's for a big get-together for Grandpop's seventy-eighth birthday. You could come as my guest."

Everyone all at once? That might be a little much, but if it was her only opportunity to meet them and let them see that she was no threat to them. "Where should I meet you?"

"I'll meet you at the ferry dock at one."

"I'll be there." She went to hang up but then stopped herself. "Wait. What's your name?"

"Hayden."

"Thank you, Hayden."

"It's your funeral, but having you come will give me something to look forward to."

❧

Rachel opened her front door and sucked in a breath. She smiled. "Christopher." Had he come back to her? Did he care so much for her that he really did forsake his family? That thought made her feel good.

"Rachel." He wore his tan designer trench coat and dress slacks.

Why hadn't she dressed better today? Jeans and a baggy sweater? "Come in."

He took in her appearance as he stepped over the threshold.

"I'll quick go change." She stopped at the touch of his hand on her arm.

"You don't have to." He slid his hand down and took her hand. "It's not the same without you. Would you please reconsider? You really got under my skin. I haven't told Father and Mother anything yet. Mother thinks you just need a little time, that you are having cold feet."

"I can't lie about my heritage." Even if they could keep it from his parents, Christopher would come to resent her. "Eventually someone would find out." Then he would hate her for destroying everything. They had to be honest with his parents from the start, or they could build nothing but a house of cards. That kind of house was never meant to last.

"Then. . ." Christopher slipped his hand from hers. "I need Mother's pearls."

Her heart dropped to her stomach with a thud, and the air was suddenly sucked from her lungs. It was really over between them if he wanted them back.

"They weren't with your other jewelry at your apartment."

He'd searched her apartment? She mentally shrugged. It didn't matter. There was nothing there that she cared all that much about. "I'll get them."

She went to her bedroom and removed the necklace and earrings from her jewelry case. She held them tight in her fist and squeezed her eyes shut. She hated to give them up, but she couldn't, in good conscience, keep them when she wouldn't be marrying him. Maybe she could change his mind. Or could she live with ignoring her heritage? Christopher's family could be her family. But what of her real heritage? She wanted to know more. She needed to know more. She fingered through the rest of her case and took out her three-karat engagement ring, a diamond tennis bracelet, a ruby pendent necklace, and matching dangle earrings.

She returned to him and dropped the pearls into his hand. She held the other jewels in her hand at her side just in case. . . in case what?

He lifted the bottom of his coat and slipped the pearls into his pants pocket.

She watched them disappear. Her heart sighed. She held open her other hand. "Here."

He stared a moment at the jewelry she held. "Keep them."

She took up his hand and dumped the contents of her hand into his.

"I bought these for you." He set them on the side table by the door. "For when you come to your senses." He put one hand behind her head and kissed her forehead, then walked out.

⁂

Rachel opened her door Saturday morning to find Will standing there. "I thought you were leaving today."

"I am." Will stepped inside and closed the door. "I wanted to wait until I knew you were up, so I could come over. Do you need anything before I leave?"

"No. I should be fine."

"I don't like you being here all alone. Garth and Lori have gone to visit family, as well."

"Actually, I'll be spending some time with family, as well."

"Really."

"I talked with my second cousin, Hayden. He's Twin Bear's grandson. The family is having a birthday party for Twin Bear's seventy-eighth birthday. Hayden invited me to come."

"That's great. So the family is welcoming to you."

"Not exactly. Charlotte and Emily both hung up on me, and Gray doesn't know I'm coming. No one knows I'm coming except Hayden. But I'm sure once they meet me, we'll work everything out."

"You are going alone into a den of people who don't want you there?" He shook his head. "I'm going with you."

"I'm sure I'll be fine."

"I'll meet you at the dock."

That's just what Hayden had said. It would be nice to be with at least one person she could count on who was glad to be with her.

eleven

Rachel disembarked the ferry on the mainland and waited by the ticket booth under the awning, just slightly out of the wind. Who would arrive first? She'd come early to make sure she didn't miss either of them, but now she wished she hadn't. The cold was biting her exposed skin.

Soon a silver sedan pulled up, and Will jumped out. "Get in. I have it warm." He opened the passenger door.

She gratefully climbed in. "I didn't realize it would be so cold out."

He turned up the heat. "The cold goes right through you." Then he drove toward the entrance of the parking lot and stopped. "We'll wait here."

"How will we know him? I forgot to ask what he looks like or how to recognize him."

"He'll probably be the only teenaged boy coming to the ferry dock alone. I think we'll know." He turned to face her. "If he shows up at all."

"You think he might not come?"

"Talk is cheap. He may have had second thoughts about taking you to the family get-together."

That was true. "Nice car. I never thought about you having one with no cars on the island. Where do you keep it?"

"It's my mom's. She lets me use it when I'm on the mainland."

"Does she live here in Mackinaw City?"

He shook his head. "She lives down the coast an hour."

"So this wasn't convenient for you to come today?"

"I wanted to be here for you."

"Well, thank you. I appreciate it.

Then Will said, "How old did you say Twin Bear was going to be today?"

"Seventy-eight."

"That has to be wrong."

"I'm sure that's what Hayden said. Positive of it."

"Dancing Turtle would have been turning seventy-eight today."

"How can that be?"

"Either one of them wasn't really turning seventy-eight today, or they are twins. It almost makes sense. If the pair of them were called Twin Bear, maybe only Dancing Turtle changed his name."

"If they didn't get along, I can understand my grandpa changing his name, but why didn't Twin Bear?"

Will shook his head. "I have no clue. It doesn't make sense to me."

He turned toward the parking lot entrance. "That's our boy." He pointed to a metallic gray minivan.

"How do you know?"

"A teen boy driving the family bus. Oh yeah. That's him."

She and Will got out, and the van pulled up beside them. A boy, about seventeen or eighteen, got out wearing only a white-striped, button-down shirt hanging open over a white T-shirt. His shaggy black hair hung over his forehead and split slightly to reveal a triangle of forehead beneath.

"Are you Hayden?"

He nodded with a smile. "And you must be Rachel, the relative nobody wants to talk to."

Will gripped her forearm. "You don't have to go through with this."

She looked up at him. "I want to."

Will held his hand out to the boy. "I'm Will Tobin."

The boy slapped Will's hand, snapped, and pointed at him.

"Hayden Dubois, eldest child of Gray and Pamela, first in line for. . .nothing." He rattled it off like it was some sort of title.

She wasn't sure what to think of him. He seemed jaded at such a young age. But somewhere inside she understood. She had felt like a nobody under her stepfathers.

"So if my grandpops and yours are brothers, then what does that make us?"

"Second cousins, I think."

"Cool." The breeze off Lake Huron ruffled his overshirt. "Aren't you cold?"

"Naw. It's not cold. You can just follow me. That way you can leave whenever they run you off."

Will spoke up. "You aren't very optimistic about this meeting."

"With my family, if they don't stab you in the back, they will eat you alive. All verbally, of course." He climbed back into his van.

Will held the door for Rachel to get into his car. When he climbed in, he said, "I don't think you should go."

"I'm sure it's not as bad as Hayden is making it out to be. You know how kids can exaggerate."

He shook his head and started the car. "I still don't like this."

They drove, following Hayden, for about a half hour east, along the northern coast of the Lower Peninsula, then exited into the town of Cheboygan.

They pulled up in front of a pale yellow house with white shutters.

Once inside, Hayden closed the door. "You can leave your coats on the railing."

Will took her coat and put it over the railing leading upstairs with his. A wave of nervousness swept over her at the thought of meeting all these people she had longed to know before she ever knew they existed. She took a deep breath, bit her bottom lip, and stepped into the living room crowded with people.

One by one, the people in the room began to stare at the pair of newcomer strangers, and the room slowly grew quiet. Hayden walked to an old man sitting in a chair by the fireplace. It must be Twin Bear. "Happy birthday, Grandpops."

"Humph. What's so happy about it? I'm going to die any day now, and then you'll all be celebrating."

"I brought you a present." Hayden motioned for Rachel to come over.

She walked slowly under the staring glares.

"Look, Grandpops."

When Twin Bear's gaze settled on her, his frown softened and his dark eyes lit up. "Charlotte? My Charlotte came back to me."

A heavy-set woman in her forties moved closer to him. "No, Pops. I'm Charlotte."

He waved a hand in her direction. "I know who you are." He pointed one misshapen finger at her. "This is my Charlotte."

Hurt shone in the woman's eyes.

"I'm not Charlotte. My name is Rachel Coe. Your brother said I'm his granddaughter."

He lowered his hand. "I don't have a brother."

"Charles Dubois. Your brother."

Charlotte leaned over and spoke near his ear.

His frown hardened again. "Thief! That's all you are. Don't think that just because you are in my house you'll get to keep it. Be gone with you. Go on. Go, before I call the police."

Charlotte gave her a triumphant sneer. "You should leave now."

"But you're my family." Wouldn't they at least give her a chance?

"No, we're not," Twin Bear snarled. "Lies. It's all lies. And

I'm going to prove it and get my house back."

He was nothing but a bitter, mean old man.

Will took her arm. "Let's go."

As she turned to exit the room, she caught sight of the little girl who had been outside her house. She looked up at her with big brown eyes that held no hint of animosity toward her. That was just the look she'd had in her dream.

Will guided her back to the front door helped her on with her coat.

"I can't believe they won't even talk to me."

"You don't need them."

Hayden came up to them. "I'm proud of you, Cuz. You lasted longer than I thought. And you stood up to Grandpops."

"Are you going to get in trouble for bringing me?"

He shrugged. "It doesn't matter."

Will opened the door, and they left. The cold air slapped her in the face. Her family really didn't want her. That just seemed unreal to her.

"That was really weird. He looked just like Dancing Turtle but with a scowl," Will said.

"So they were twins?"

Gray Dubois came out the front door swinging his coat on. "Pops and Uncle Charles grew up in that house. You should know he wants it back."

"Can he take it from me?"

He just looked at her.

She squared her shoulders. "I'm staying in my house whether or not any of you believe I'm Charles Dubois's granddaughter."

He shrugged.

She turned to Will. "I don't want to lose my house."

"It doesn't really matter if you are related to Dancing Turtle or not. The house belonged to him free and clear, and he gave it to you. He could have given it to the little old lady from Pasadena, and no one could take it from her."

It was good to know her house was safe. She turned back to Gray. "One more thing. Hayden said that when my grandmother left she was pregnant with one of the brothers' baby—that would be my mom. Who is my grandfather? Charles or Lewis?"

"I really don't know."

"What if Lewis is really my grandfather?"

"Then my dad's bitter existence will be that much more cruel."

⁂

Will drove her back to the ferry. "Are you sure you want to go back to the island? Mom would be happy to make room for you."

She just wanted to be alone for a while. "I have a lot to do back at the house." She got out of the car and walked to the handful of people waiting for the incoming ferry.

Will turned to face her. "I hate to leave you alone after that rejection."

"You did warn me after all." She just never imagined their rejection would be so complete. A tear slipped down her cheek. "I just thought if they could see me that maybe they would accept me." Another tear.

Will put his arms around her and pulled her close. "I'm sorry it didn't turn out the way you wanted."

She leaned into him. At least someone cared. "I just wanted a family. To belong. To have a heritage." A sob choked her last word.

"No one can take your heritage away from you."

She cried against his coat for a minute. "How could they not want part of their family?"

"They've been hurt."

"So they hurt others?"

"Sometimes people do that." He leaned slightly away from her to look her in the face but kept his arms around her. "I'm sorry you had to go through that."

The compassion in his eyes told her that he truly was. The concern quickly turned to longing, and he lowered his head toward hers.

Just as his lips were about to touch hers, she pushed away. "That's not going to help anything." She could see disappointment in his eyes.

"I could return Mom's car and head back to the island myself so you won't be alone."

"I may not even stay on the island over the holidays." She wasn't sure why she said that. She just didn't want Will to ruin his holiday because of her, didn't want to deny him his family because she had none. She didn't know what she was going to do. Maybe she would go back to Boston. "You go back to your mom's, and I'll be fine."

"I'll call you tonight and see how you are doing."

"Will, you are not responsible for me. Don't go changing your life for me."

"Can't I be concerned about a friend?"

"Friend?"

He nodded. "Sure. Just friends." Then he dug a piece of paper out of his coat pocket and wrote something on the back. "Here's my mom's number. If you need anything at all, don't hesitate to call."

"I can't do this right now."

He still held the paper. "Can't do what?"

"Whatever it is we are doing here—this back-and-forth thing. I don't want you to think there is something going on between us. I need to sort out my feelings about Christopher and being Native American." She sighed. "And my family not wanting anything to do with me. I can't be worrying about what is going on between us, too. I just need some time."

He put the paper in her hand and wrapped her fingers around it. "I just want to be your friend, in whatever capacity you need me. I promise I won't try to push beyond that. Just friends."

He was being friendly, but she sensed it was more than friends he wanted to be. She didn't want to deal with that right now, so she just nodded.

⁊

That evening, Rachel sat on her couch with her knees held tightly to her chest alone and lonely. Lori and her husband had left the island to visit Garth's family for the Christmas holiday. Will was gone visiting family over his break. The only family she had didn't want anything to do with her. Except for maybe Hayden, but he was just a kid. Will had warned her, but still she had hoped.

God, if You really do exist, why did You make me this way? Why do I have to be part Native American? My life was so simple before.

She let the tears fall. Suddenly she sat up straight and forced her tears to cease. She could tell Christopher she had reconsidered. Had come to her senses. She walked to her bedroom and slipped on her engagement ring. If her family here didn't want her, she would go where she was wanted.

She went to the phone. She held the receiver in her hand and stared at the buttons. What should she say? She didn't know. Maybe it would be best just to let the words come. But all she could do was stare at the numbers. Her family may not want her, but truthfully, she didn't want to go back to Christopher either. She hung up the phone and took off the ring.

She looked at the bag by the entry table that had the Bible in it that Will had given her. She took it out of the bag and set it on the empty coffee table, then stared at it. *What possible good could reading it do?*

She stood and walked around her cozy little living room. The heap of papers she had quickly scooped up when

Christopher had dropped in still lay in a mess in the chair.

She hadn't been up to sorting through any more of the information her grandfather had collected after Christopher had come. . .and left her. It all seemed useless anyway. None of it seemed to be important and nothing connected. What was the point to any of it? If she only had a rough sketch of her family tree, she might be able to begin to put some of the pieces together. Right now it seemed as though each piece went to a different puzzle. Why couldn't her grandfather have been more organized?

If she was ever going to get the answers she sought, she would need to dive back into it, but she just didn't feel like it right now.

She picked up the Bible and curled up on the couch. She didn't believe in the Bible or a personal God. Maybe some all-powerful being out there watched her squirm like a bug under a microscope—a being that would demand perfection from her.

There was a sticky note sticking out from the side of the Bible that said, *Start here.* Start in the middle? She opened up to that place, and on the hidden part of the sticky note it said, *Read the book of John.*

Okay, Will. I'll read this, but it won't change my mind.

She stood and took the Bible to her room and dressed for bed. She always preferred reading in bed. Once all snuggled beneath the covers, she opened the Bible again and read about a charismatic man who only had to ask and men followed him without concern to their former life. A man who performed miracle after miracle and never did anything wrong. A good man. An innocent man who died a senseless death.

She slammed the book shut when Jesus gave up His Spirit on the cross. "He died! How unfair was that?" Somewhere in the back of her memory, she'd learned that He was crucified, but this was such an awful and brutal death. She wasn't reading another word. Make her care about this man then let him die like that!

She put the Bible aside and turned off the light. She punched her pillow. What was the point in believing in some great man if he was dead? How could that help her? Jesus did everything right, and God just let Him die.

She jerked the chain on the lamp beside her bed and sat up, glaring at the Bible. "God—if You exist—why would You let Your Son die? I don't understand." She flipped open the Bible to the beginning of John. Will had highlighted a few verses throughout the book. There was one in particular she wanted to find again. She didn't have far to go when she found it, chapter three verse sixteen.

"For God so loved the world that He gave His one and only Son, that whoever believes in Him shall not perish but have eternal life."

"How come Jesus had to perish, but You would give me eternal life? He was Your only Son!"

She flipped through more pages until she found the spot where Jesus said He was going to prepare a place and He would come back to get the men who had been with Him. Was this some sort of afterlife? Maybe Jesus didn't really die.

She flipped back to the place where Jesus died and continued reading. Just as Jesus had said to His men that they would mourn and then have joy, she felt joy when Jesus rose from the dead.

His resurrection was different from the resurrections of Lazarus and the girl whom Jesus had raised from the dead. While they were brought back to life as a testimony to Jesus' power, they later faced physical death again. If Rachel interpreted what she had read correctly, Jesus had conquered death forever—both physically and spiritually.

How could Will's God love her when no one else could? How could an all-powerful perfect being love someone imperfect like her? Maybe when she fixed herself and got herself perfect, the God who would give up His Son for her could accept her.

❧

A week and a half later, Rachel wished she had taken the Bible Will had given her with her back to her Boston apartment. Though the passages he marked were confusing, somehow they were also comforting. She had given her notice to her landlord, and he was able to rent the apartment to another tenant as soon as she could get her things moved out.

She was almost through and had just taped the last box to go to charity, when the doorbell rang. She was surprised to see Christopher's mother on the other side of her door. "Emma. Would you like to come in?" Not that she thought she would.

Emma smiled and stepped inside.

Both gestures surprised her. "Would you like something to drink? I only have bottled water."

"No, I'm fine, dear." Emma took off her sable fur coat and draped it over a stack of boxes. "So you are really leaving."

"There's no point in me having two places."

"So that's all there is to it?"

Huh?

"I've come on behalf of Christopher. He's been a wreck since you left, like a lost little kitten. What can we do to get you to reconsider?"

"Reconsider? Exactly what did Christopher tell you about our break up?"

"That there was some misunderstanding about the house you inherited."

"Misunderstanding? No. Everything is quite clear." Poor Christopher. He still hadn't told his parents. He couldn't admit that she was part Native American, Ojibwa—couldn't bring himself to say it aloud. Well, she would do what he couldn't admit. "My grandfather who left me the house was Ojibwa."

Emma's smile tightened. "I don't know what that is, dear."

"Native American. What you would call an Indian."

Emma's countenance fell as though she'd just been insulted. "That can't be. You look so European."

People saw what they wanted to see. "I am the very thing you and your family loathe." They would never truly accept her. She knew that now, and Emma was about to prove it.

Emma stared at her a moment, then collected her coat and left.

The act spelled the end of her connection with the Winstons. As Rachel thought about all the implications of that, she realized she felt more relieved than disappointed. No more acting perfect, wondering when they would find out she had flaws. In her twenty-five years she had learned that everyone had flaws. Some people were simply more adept at hiding them.

twelve

Will had returned early from winter break, arriving two days after Christmas. He hated the idea of Rachel being alone in her house with no one she could call who could come in a hurry. But she hadn't been there. She had really left the island as she said she was going to.

Now, two days before New Year's Eve, she was back. He'd been contemplating for the last two hours, since she stepped off a taxi sleigh, whether or not to go over and welcome her home. She might not be too happy to see him after their last encounter on the dock. Then again, there was nothing wrong with a neighbor greeting another neighbor. He put on his coat and trudged through the snow across the street.

He took a deep breath before she opened the door so he could get his hello out before she closed the door in his face. "I just wanted to welcome you back." He held up both his hands in front of himself. "I promise, I'm here only as a friend."

She opened the door wider. "Come in out of the cold."

He unzipped his coat but left it on. "I wasn't sure you'd talk to me."

"Why?"

"The last time I saw you it didn't go so well."

She grimaced. "That was a bad day." She held out her hands to him. "Can I take your coat?"

This was a good thing, a very good thing. He handed it to her, then, while her back was turned, he allowed himself to break into a big smile.

"I just heated water. Would you like some tea or cocoa?"

"Cocoa would be great."

"Have a seat." She went to the kitchen and returned a minute later, handing him a mug. She tucked one foot under her and sat on the other end of the couch from him. "I wanted to thank you for the Bible."

He opened his mouth to protest but stopped when she held up her hand. "Before you try to deny it again, I have proof." She set her tea on the coffee table and handed him the Bible, opening it to where he'd stuck the sticky note at the beginning of John. That wasn't proof.

She unfolded a piece of paper and laid it on top of the open Bible. "It's the same handwriting." It was the paper he'd written the contact information for Twin Bear's family.

He knew he should have typed it. Busted. He had to smile. "So did you read any of it?"

"I did." She picked up her tea mug and took a sip.

"And."

"What I don't understand is why an all-powerful God would send His only Son to die for a world that really doesn't like Him?"

Questions were good. They showed interest. "Because He loves us that much, even though we don't deserve it."

"It still doesn't make sense. No one would make that kind of sacrifice."

"Exactly. No human would, but God would. He has done everything to save us. Becoming a Christian is to be adopted into God's family. In biblical times, adoption was permanent. You could disown a biological child but not an adopted one. All we have to do is believe, accept his Son as our savior."

"I guess."

He waited. "So?"

"So what?"

She was ready. He could feel it. "Do you want me to pray with you to become a Christian?"

"I don't think so."

He almost let his jaw fall open but caught himself before it did. "But you are so ready."

"Obviously not."

"But. . .but. . ." He sounded like an idiot. "What if something happens to you tonight, heaven forbid, and you die before you have another chance to accept Jesus as your savior and go to heaven? The alternative is not pretty."

"What could possibly happen to me on this quiet little island tonight?"

"I don't know. You could be plugging in your toaster and get electrocuted."

"I don't eat toast. And if I did, I'd make sure to not have any tonight."

"You could have a heart attack or seizure."

"I'm perfectly healthy."

"Your house could burn down."

"Or a tidal wave could come or a meteor might land on me. I'll be fine for the night."

He hoped so.

Will returned home and went to bed, but he got up again at one fifteen and paced around his house.

Lord, please protect Rachel. Don't let anything bad happen to her tonight. Give me another chance to get through to her.

Not settled enough to go back to bed, he knelt beside his bed. This was becoming a habit, being on his knees. *Lord, please bring her to You, even if she never speaks to me again. She'll talk to me in heaven.*

❧

Rachel flipped over once again in her bed and fluffed her pillow. She kept hearing Will's words. *What if something happens to you?* Finally, she succumbed to sleep.

At one thirty, she woke with a start. Was that smoke she smelled? She was sure it was and clicked on her light and walked through the house. Nothing appeared to be on fire, and now she couldn't smell anything. She could swear she had smelled smoke.

She climbed back into bed but just sat there trying to smell the smoke again. What if there was a fire in the walls? Who knows how old this house was? The wiring could go bad, and she would never know it until it was too late.

Your house could catch on fire.

The words echoing in her head startled her, and she pulled her knees up to her chest.

God, I don't want something to happen to me and not go to heaven. I'm afraid to wait a moment longer. It's way too late to call Will for help, so I'm calling You. You're still up, right? What do I do?

I know I'm not perfect and I do wrong things all the time, but You say You love me anyway. I know You sent Your Son Jesus to die because of my wrong things. Please make me a Christian like Will.

A peace and warmth and love washed over her. She couldn't keep from grinning. *Was that it, Lord? Did I do it?*

She snuggled back down in her covers with a sigh and drifted right back to sleep.

ஐ

The next day giddiness bubbled up inside her. She couldn't ever remember being this happy and couldn't wait for Will to come over. What time did he get up anyway? Could she wait that long? His drapes were still shut. If she didn't tell someone, she would burst. She had awoken early, yet more rested than she could ever remember. Considering her middle-of-the-night house-roamings in search of a phantom fire, this surprised her.

An hour later, Will arrived to help her sort through the papers again. He made sure to let her know, once again, he was over as "just a friend."

He stood in the office next to a box, staring up at her blank wall and rubbed his hands together. "Your wall is kind of bare. Let's do something about that."

She'd been excited to tell him about last night, but now she wasn't sure what had happened. Had anything? What if it was all just a dream or hoax?

"What's wrong?"

"Huh?" She focused her gaze on him.

Will's brown eyes were searching her face. "You have a funny expression."

"I was just wondering what exactly do you have to pray to become a Christian?"

"I was hoping you'd be open to this discussion. There isn't an exact prayer, but you have to admit you are a sinner. . ."

She'd done that.

". . .acknowledge Jesus is the Son of God. . ."

She'd done that, too. An excitement bubbled up inside her.

". . .and that He died for your sins."

And that, too! "Is that all?"

"Basically. If you have any other questions, I'd be happy to answer them the best that I can. If not, would you like me to pray with you? Sometimes that's easier."

She could feel her mouth spread into a wide grin. "No need. I did all that last night."

His eyes widened. "Really."

She nodded emphatically.

"That's fantastic." He reached over and gave her a big congratulatory hug.

She pulled back after a moment, but he kept his arms around her and looked deep into her eyes. Something was passing between them. But what? He cleared his throat. "Still friends?"

She felt that was best for now and nodded. He stepped away from her. An awkwardness settled between them.

Maybe she could dispel it with a little conversation. "It was the weirdest thing. I woke up at one thirty with a start as if someone had shaken me out of my sleep, and I could smell smoke. Remember what you said about my house catching fire? I could have sworn I smelled smoke, but when I looked around the house I couldn't find any trace of fire, and I could no longer smell the smoke. I was afraid to die and not go to heaven, so I asked God to save me."

His smile grew as she told her story.

"Why are you smiling?"

"Prayer works."

"Pardon?" The earlier awkwardness was gone.

"I crawled out of bed about one fifteen and couldn't go back to sleep, so I got down on my knees and was praying for you. I'm afraid the smoke smell might have been my fault, though I didn't specifically pray for smoke."

"Are you saying it was somehow God or something?"

"If I had to bet on God or on the something, I'd go with God. It is no coincidence that I was praying for you at the same time you smelled smoke and prayed for salvation. It was almost two o'clock when I felt at peace and was able to go back to sleep. What time did you go back to bed?"

This was really weird. She opened her mouth, but the words caught in her throat. She cleared it. "About two o'clock."

"I'd definitely go with God. He does work in mysterious ways."

"So what do I do now?"

"Church is always a great place to start. Read little bits of your Bible every day and pray."

"What if I don't understand something? Can I ask you?"

"Of course. But you don't have to wait for me. If you don't understand something, ask God to reveal it to you. He'll help you. He wants you to understand His Word. That is why He has made sure it has survived for thousands of years."

"Should I just start at the beginning? What you had me read was way past the middle."

"You can start anywhere you want, but the New Testament

is usually easier for most young Christians to understand."

She wanted to learn everything God had to say right now.

"So what you said last night about being part of God's family. Am I part of that family now?"

"Definitely. Now and forever."

thirteen

"I'm almost ready," Rachel said as she pushed her feet into her black snow boots.

He just liked watching her, being around her. Was her becoming a Christian his cue to move forward, beyond friendship, into a romantic relationship with her? He wanted to, but something was still holding him back. He wasn't sure she was ready for that step. He took her coat off the tree rack and held it for her.

She slipped her arms into it. "Don't you think it's odd that Lori and Garth invited us over together?"

"Maybe." It was a bit strange. Both Lori and Garth knew they weren't a "couple." They didn't even know Rachel had become a Christian.

As far as he knew, Garth and Lori had only just gotten back from winter break earlier today, and he and Garth would be going back to work tomorrow. Garth was insistent they come tonight. It couldn't wait. What couldn't wait until tomorrow? And why did Rachel have to come as well? He was glad she was coming. He liked being with her. He would take any excuse.

They stepped out into the cold night air. Light snow drifted from the sky. He would likely find an inch or two by morning for his trip to school.

"*Brr.* It's cold out here." Rachel hunched her shoulders.

He wanted to put his arm around her but shoved his hands deep into his pockets instead. They were just friends. . .for now. "It's supposed to get colder as the week wears on."

"It's not cold enough already?" Rachel pushed her hands

deeper into her coat pockets. "What do you think this is about tonight?"

"I don't know. Garth just said they had a surprise."

"Do you think they are going to announce that they are pregnant?"

"Uh, Rachel. It's best if you don't bring that up. It's a sensitive topic for Lori. Garth told me that she was in a serious car accident as a kid and can't have children."

"That's so sad. Is Garth okay with that?"

"Sure. He's so crazy about her, she could have third eye and it would be fine with him."

She chuckled.

"He says that they will just spend their whole lives being on their honeymoon."

She looked at him sideways. "What about you? Do you want to have kids some day?"

He held his breath for a moment. Why was she asking him about kids? Was she searching for a specific answer? He swallowed hard. "Sure. I guess so." He turned toward her. "But I don't have to." Noncommittal, he could go either way that way. "What about you? You want kids?"

"I'm not sure. My childhood was a little battered. I don't know if I'd want to put a child through that. It doesn't seem fair just to satisfy some internal desire."

"Not all childhoods have to be battered." Arriving at Garth and Lori's door cut the topic short for better or for worse.

Before he could knock, Garth swung the door open and called, "They're here."

He still had to wonder what this was all about. Rachel had been right that this was unusual. Garth had a grin bigger than he'd ever seen. Then Garth stood between him and Rachel and draped an arm over each of their shoulders. "We want you two to be the first on the island to meet our children."

Lori walked out of one of the bedrooms with her arms

around two redheaded children. The boy about seven and the girl looked to be three or four.

Garth pointed. "That's Michael, and that's Lindy. Short for Melinda."

Lindy turned and held her arms up to Lori who picked her up. "She's a little shy."

Garth went over and scooped up Michael.

Later, when Will had a moment alone with Garth, he asked, "Are they really yours?"

Garth glanced over at his wife and new children. "They sure are."

Seeing the pride on Garth's face pulled at his own paternal instinct. An instinct he didn't think he had. "How? Where did they come from?"

"Their parents were killed in a car accident. We knew about this before the break, but Lori wanted to keep it to ourselves in case things didn't work out. We met them over Thanksgiving. That's why Lori didn't come back with me."

Rachel was talking to Lori who again held Lindy. Did those kids do anything to Rachel like they were doing to him? He suddenly realized that what he said earlier was in error. He definitely wanted children. Would Rachel change her heart as well?

When he was walking her home, he decided to bring up the topic of children again. "Michael and Lindy sure were cute."

"They were. But then other people's children usually are."

"They didn't make you want to have your own children?"

"I don't think I'd make a good mom."

"Why not?"

"I don't see juggling a modeling career and motherhood as being compatible."

"You could always take some time off."

"I suppose. Fortunately it is not something I have to think about right now."

He wanted to ask her if she had planned to have children with her ex after they were married, but they arrived at her door. He should just let it go for now.

Rachel stood inside the doorway. "Do you want to come in for a little while?"

Though it was still early, he shook his head. "I need to get ready for work tomorrow." And he had some thinking to do.

He stood in his darkened living room looking across the street at Rachel's house. If he wanted children and she didn't, was there any point in pursuing a relationship that might eventually end because of different goals for their lives? He could save himself a lot of heartache if he just ended it now. But how? He'd tried to forget about her before when he'd found out she was engaged. Besides, his heart was too far gone to save him emotional heartache.

He let his thoughts drift into the future. What if he ended up with Rachel and no children? Could he be content, as Garth had been, simply to spend his life as a honeymooner without children? Or would he rather end up with someone else and have children? He shook his head. Who else? In his twenty-eight years, no one had ever touched his heart the way Rachel had done. And she wasn't even trying. He might very well end up as a bachelor the rest of his life, like Dancing Turtle. He'd have his students at school, but he'd always come home alone to an empty house.

Lord, If I am to pursue a relationship with Rachel, make it clear to me. Help me to determine Your will and accept it, whatever it may be.

fourteen

A week and a half later, Rachel again sat on the floor of her office, an open box between her and Will. They never made much progress, but she enjoyed his company. She should really pack for leaving for Europe tomorrow. She didn't need much, though, and could just throw some stuff into a suitcase.

When Will had come again today, he'd made sure to tell her he was here just as a friend. She appreciated him making sure that was clear so she didn't have to wonder, but she had told him he didn't have to say it every time he came over and that she would just assume their status was friendship until otherwise stated. She liked having him as a friend.

She pulled a newspaper article out of the box. "This one might be on my grandmother's side of the family. What do you think?" She held it out to him.

He didn't take it. "Just put it in the empty box."

"Shouldn't we catalog it, so we can find it again?"

"I don't think we need to bother with it right now."

"How come every time I want to do something with information I think might be related to my grandmother, you tell me not to bother?"

"I just think we should focus on Dancing Turtle's family."

Rachel swallowed against a rising irritation. "Why? Because he is male and the male lineage is the only one that matters?"

"No."

"Then what is it?"

"I just think the Ojibwa connection is more interesting."

"But I have family on both sides. I can't ignore one side because it might be boring." Was he just like Christopher, only acknowledging what was acceptable? She made a special pile for it. She wouldn't toss it aside.

The silence that followed irritated her. She wanted the easy camaraderie they usually had. And Ojibwa was just the way to get it back. "If I'm at least one-quarter Ojibwa and whatever else, what are you?"

"What does that matter?"

"I just want to know. Are you all Ojibwa?"

"No."

"Then what?"

He shrugged. "I don't know."

"I find that hard to believe—you, who knows the island history better than anyone." What was the big deal?

Flustered, he said, "I have some French and English I guess."

"How much?"

He raised his voice a little. "What does it matter?"

"I guess it matters to you, or you wouldn't be trying to hide it."

"I'm not hiding it."

Let him believe what he wanted. Just like Christopher's family, he molded his heritage to suit him. "You seem to be only interested in Native American things. Is that the only reason you are friends with me, because I'm part Ojibwa?"

"No. Of course not."

"Then what?"

He scratched his head. "I don't know. I can't think of anything off the top of my head. Sometimes there aren't specific reasons. It just is."

"And sometimes it's Ojibwa blood."

He frowned then turned and walked out.

Fine. She'd had enough of his surly mood for one day.

❧

Will kicked into the middle of his living room one of his

dress shoes he'd taken off after school. Why couldn't he have just given a simple answer and not gotten upset over it? He hated his other ancestry. Hated to think about, hated to admit it. Why couldn't he just be full-blood Ojibwa?

He envied Rachel for wanting to embrace her whole heritage. The good and the bad. She wanted Twin Bear's family even though they didn't want her. They didn't deserve her.

Lord, why can't I be full-blood? Why do I have to be mixed? Why couldn't You give me ancestors to be proud of?

He pulled out a paper his younger sister had written in sixth grade, when all that mattered was that she had a famous ancestor—if only on a local level. Back then, she had refused to be ashamed of either her Native American heritage or her infamous European ancestors. She had gotten some teasing on both accounts but just held her head up and ignored them—unlike himself. As a boy, he'd been expected to fight to defend his family's honor or prove his worth. Instead, he'd just put his head down in shame.

Why, Lord?

Suddenly, a sermon he'd heard years ago forced its way to the front of his mind. It was on the importance of lineage, in particular, Jesus' lineage. All those names were recorded to prove He was the prophesied Messiah. The pastor had pointed out that it did show that Jesus was a descendant of King David, but it also revealed that He was descended from a prostitute, murderer, and thief, as well as His divine lineage. Jesus had scoundrels in His line. *Just like me.*

He smiled. He'd lost sight of the fact—or maybe he'd never seen—how God was not ashamed of Will's heritage. It didn't matter so much who was in his lineage, but how he behaved. How he pleased God.

He touched his choker. Is this what Dancing Turtle meant by "finding his way?" Had Dancing Turtle sensed what he'd been hiding from?

Will pulled up next to Garth in the teachers' "parking lot." He'd wished he'd been able to talk to Rachel before she left for Europe. Make amends for his poor behavior. Explain to her about his ancestors.

Garth shook his head at some of the students parking their snowmobiles. "I still can't get over kids that young driving to school."

"They can get a snowmobile license at twelve." It had taken him a bit to get used to it, too.

"Garth do you think the only reason I like Rachel is because of her Ojibwa heritage?"

"No."

That was an answer but not very helpful. "How can you be sure?"

"Isn't Stacy one of the few people around here who is almost full-blooded Native American?"

"I've heard she's close." He tucked his helmet under his arm and headed for the door.

"Are you attracted to her?"

Stacy was cute, and he'd taken her out once, but there was no energy between them. No spark. "What does my lack of attraction to Stacy have to do with Rachel?"

Garth held the door open for him. "If you were only interested in Rachel because she is part Ojibwa, then wouldn't it stand to reason that you would be more attracted to Stacy because she has a stronger Native American background?"

There was a degree of logic there. So then why did he like her? "Your wife still thinks I like Rachel because she's beautiful."

"You may have initially been attracted to her because of her looks, as I was with Lori, but you've spent a lot of time with her. If she were shallow and uninteresting, you wouldn't want to be around her. You'd be bored."

She definitely didn't bore him. She captivated him with her passion for the past. He loved history. He wanted to understand how her mind worked. Her organizational style was definitely unique. He would guess she was a visual learner. That was why she liked to spread everything out and tape things to the wall. He'd tried to get her to put everything in neat orderly files where she could find things easily, but she kept pulling everything back out.

He missed her. When was she coming back? She'd said she would be gone for two weeks. That didn't tell him what day she would return. Exactly two weeks? Just shy of two weeks? A little over two weeks?

He wanted to kiss her, but even more, he wanted to be her friend. He'd said they were friends, and he was going to stick to that until he got a leading from God to move forward. *Remember, Lord, I'm a little dense sometimes. You're going to have to knock me over the head with it if You don't want me to mess it up.*

❧

Will sat on the couch with his mom as the end credits to the movie they'd just watched rolled up the screen. He should head to bed.

His mom picked up the remote and turned off the TV. "When are you going to bring Rachel home for a visit so I can get to know her better?"

He cocked his mouth up on one side. "When I get around to asking her out."

"The way you talk about her, I thought you'd been dating for some time now."

"Things were complicated at first."

"And now?"

"I'm waiting for clear direction from the Lord."

"Are you serious about her?"

"Pretty serious." He wouldn't be spending so much time with her if he weren't.

"Then I have something for you." She left the room and returned a moment later. "I've known since your dad died that I would pass this on to you." She put something into his hand.

He lifted the ring out of his palm. "This is your wedding ring." A white gold band with a diamond in the raised center and a plain matching wedding band thinner in width.

"It is for you to give to the woman you decide to marry. Whether that is Rachel or another woman."

Was that a hint? His vote was for Rachel. Would Rachel be happy with a ring this conservative? "What about Mandy, Bethany, and Lauren?"

"Mandy has hers from Jake, and your other sisters will receive their rings from their fiancés one day. You are my only son. I want you to have mine. My heart told me that now was the right time to give it to you."

Was this his sign to move forward in his relationship with Rachel? He just wasn't sure.

fifteen

Rachel sat with her eyes closed as the make-up artist fussed with the shadow on her eyelids. Curlers in her hair waited for the stylist. Mark still had not told her what she would be wearing for today's shoot.

This was the last shoot of the European tour. This one, Mark had said would be special and the best of all. They were shooting at the ruins of a castle in England. She would have three dress, make-up, and hair changes today. It was going to be a long day.

People gave models all the credit for the end result, when in reality, the model was only the canvas for the make-up artist, hair stylist, and clothing designer to show off their talents, and the photographer captured it all on film or, these days, a digital memory card. But they seemed to get fewer accolades. The model became famous, and the others were forgotten. It didn't seem fair.

She had enjoyed her five-country tour of Europe, but she kept longing for home, for Mackinac Island. She kept wondering what Will was doing. Things were so unsettled between them.

Mitzy finished with her eyes. "Keep them closed." Then she dusted her face and blew gently to remove any excess.

"Can I open now?"

After a moment of silence, Mitzy said, "Oops, go ahead and open. You can't see me nod with your eyes closed, can you?"

She blinked against the light.

Mitzy aimed for her lips with a small lip brush. The last touch. "So when are you moving back to Boston?"

She waited for Mitzy to dab the brush in more color before

answering. "I don't know. Maybe never."

Mitzy stared at her with her jaw unhinged, her brush hanging in the air between them. "You can't *not* live in Boston. What about Mark?"

"There are plenty of other models for him to shoot." And she could still travel to shoots and even work with Mark from time to time.

"I just assumed that the two of you would be getting back together, now that Christopher was out of the picture."

"Mark and I were never *together* to begin with, so there would be no getting back together. He's a great photographer but hardly my type. He acknowledges me as a model, but he has always been interested in Tansy."

"Tansy Rockford?"

She nodded.

"She is way out of his league."

"I don't know." If a top Boston model could be interested a high-school teacher, why not Mark and Tansy?

Mitzy finished brushing the color to her lips. "So if you're not going to move back, what are you going to do?"

"For now I'll stay on Mackinac Island."

"What does that silly island have that Boston doesn't have?"

Will's face jumped to Rachel's mind, and a smile pulled at her lips. She missed him. She hated that they had fought just before she left and didn't get to resolve it.

"Or should I say *who*? What's his name?"

There was no sense denying it. "Will. He's my neighbor across the street."

"What does he look like?"

"Long dark hair pulled back into a ponytail and inviting brown eyes. A strong warrior face, yet it has a gentleness."

"Is it serious?"

In a way, yes, but not the way Mitzy meant. "We're just friends."

"Yeah, right."

But they were. He'd been so sweet since Christmas. Never pushing. Truly being her friend. "Can I look now?" Mitzy had her turned away from the mirror.

"Not until Pierre fixes your hair, and we have you in that dress. You know Mark likes you to see the whole picture on your first look, so you can be wowed by it."

Yes, but that didn't stop her from asking, and sometimes Mitzy would give her a peek. Mitzy had done something extra with her make-up, she could tell because it took her longer than usual, and she fussed more to get it right.

Pierre primped her hair, then she was put into a white iridescent gown without messing her hair or face.

Mitzy led her out of the dressing area to where Mark waited, biting his thumbnail. "Here she is."

Mark turned and pressed his hands flat together. "Yes! Perfect."

She was far from perfect and was glad she didn't have to pretend to be anymore, but everyone had obviously achieved the look he was going for.

He motioned toward a full-length mirror. "Take a look."

She sucked in a breath. "Wow."

❧

The sleigh taxi came to a stop in front of her house. She sighed. *Home.* When she looked down from the taxi to get her footing so she could get off, Will stood there with one hand extended to her. She was glad that he obviously wasn't too put off by their fight before she left.

She smiled and took it. "Thank you."

He walked her in and set her suitcase by the door.

She was too tired for company. She didn't want him to think she wasn't glad to see him, so how did she gracefully tell him to leave? "Will, I can't even begin to tell you the depth of my gratitude for you carrying that in, but I'm so exhausted I seriously don't know how I'm still standing. I don't mean to be rude, but if you don't mind, I'm going to say good night."

He nodded and moved toward the open door, reluctant to leave. "I understand. Are you still going to church in the morning?"

That's right. It was still Saturday. What an extremely long day! She leaned on the edge of the door for support, putting her cheek against the wood. "Would you give me a wake-up call?"

He smiled then. "Sure. See you in the morning."

That would give her plenty of time to sleep. She hadn't been able to attend church while she was in Europe. She missed going. "Morning it is."

"I have something for you."

A gift? He must not be harboring any ill feelings. "Can it wait until morning?"

"Sure. I'll bring it over after church."

She relished the excuse to see him more.

૪

The ringing phone startled Rachel out of a dead sleep. She gasped for air. She shook the fog from her head and stared at the clock, willing the numbers to focus. It was morning already? She stumbled to the kitchen. "Hello."

"Heavy sleeper?"

"Will?"

"This is the second time I called. I was getting worried."

"I guess I was more sleep deprived than I thought."

"The taxi comes in a half an hour. Is that enough time?"

"I'll be ready. Thanks." After all she didn't have to be perfect. Will had seen her almost at her worst.

She still needed a fast shower and a quick breakfast. But she could do it. Just because she'd never gotten ready that fast before didn't mean anything. She didn't want to miss church.

She was pulling on the pants of her pantsuit when there was a knock on the door. She pulled them up and went to the door. "Will, I just need thirty seconds to find my shoes." She went to her room and came back with one shoe on and her pantsuit jacket half on. She hobbled to the kitchen as Will took her winter coat off the coat tree. She grabbed her yogurt with a spoon handle sticking out of the top from off of the counter. She hobbled into her other shoe. "Ready."

Will held up her coat.

She slipped one arm into her coat and shifted her yogurt to her other hand. "What are you smiling about?"

"Just you rushing around."

"I made it, didn't I?"

"That's what is so amazing. I didn't think any woman could get ready that fast."

"Posh. That's just a stereotype." She headed out to the taxi and climbed into the seat behind Lori and Garth and their two new children. Will sat in the seat next to her.

Seeing Lori and Garth with their children snuggled next to them caused something inside her to pull as if constricted. She wanted that, too, which surprised her. She had been happy with her career, but now she knew it would never be enough. That is what she had been feeling in Europe, a dissatisfaction. Modeling wasn't enough any longer.

Before leaving for Europe, she'd spend most of her mornings over at Lori's house with Lori and Lindy. The little girl had become comfortable around her. Rachel even had two "drawings" stuck on her refrigerator that Lindy had given her. One scribble drawing was of Lindy's cat, the other, all pink and purple, was of Rachel. While she was in Europe, Rachel bought Lindy a doll and Michael a toy car. She would give the gifts to them after church.

Will leaned closer to her. "I know you were rushed, but you look beautiful."

His compliment made her smile and warmth coiled around her heart. "Thank you."

❧

Will sat on Rachel's porch, flipping a small yellow book back and forth in his hands. Where could she be? He'd told her he'd be over soon. He stood when he saw her walking down the street toward him.

Her eyes widened when she saw him. "Have you been waiting long?"

About twenty minutes. "No. Not long." He wanted to ask where she'd been but didn't want to sound domineering or overbearing like she had to account to him for her every move. "You take a walk?"

"I was just over at Lori and Garth's. I brought something back from Europe for the kids."

That was surprising, considering how she felt about having children. "How very thoughtful of you."

She opened her door. "Before I left I got to know Lindy. She's a real cutie. I saw this doll and had to get it for her. I couldn't bring something back for her and not her brother."

"Sounds like maybe you've become attached to her."

"I guess I have. She makes me wonder what it could be like to have kids of my own one day."

He tried not to smile too broadly. He didn't want her to know how happy that made him. Was that the hurdle they needed to cross before diving into a relationship? He sensed it wasn't. But what then? He would just have to give it a little more time. . .and prayer.

Will held out the little yellow book to her. It was a Native American history of the local tribes written by Chief Blackbird. "Open to page twenty-four."

She took it and opened it. Near the bottom of the page he'd highlighted a name. "Alvin Coe?" she whispered.

"He was a traveling missionary from Ohio in 1840."

"Do you think I'm related to him?"

"That's hard to say. It sounds like he went back to Ohio,

but anything could have happened after that. He could have returned or, maybe, one of his descendants or relatives."

She held the book out to him. "I'll have to see if I can find out anymore information on him to see if I'm related."

"Keep the book. I can easily get another."

"Thank you."

"I'm really sorry you felt like I was slighting Charlotte's side of the family. I wasn't doing it on purpose."

She shrugged. "Don't worry about it."

"I have spent all my teenaged and adult life focusing solely on my Ojibwa heritage. I forget I have other ancestors."

"You don't have to explain anything to me."

But he did. If he ever hoped to have a lasting relationship with her. "I have some pretty unsavory ancestors in my French and British lineage."

She folded her arms across her chest. "You don't have to doctor your heritage to be acceptable."

Her defense stance chilled him. "I haven't doctored it. I just try to hide from it."

"What's the difference? Change it, ignore it. It's still not the truth."

Ouch. That put him in his place. "I can hardly be proud of murders and traitors, can I?"

"You don't have to be proud of them, but hiding from them doesn't negate the fact you are still related to them. And *all* your French and British ancestors couldn't be bad."

It was just that the bad ones stuck out. "My family has their own personal Benedict Arnold. He told the British just where to land on Mackinac Island and how to take the fort. I grew up being teased and some kids wouldn't be friends with me. They would say that they were afraid I'd turn on them like Eduard Gilbert who turned on the Americans whom he'd befriended. And there have been others. I come from a long line of scoundrels."

"And I come from a long line of people who want nothing to do with me. Aren't we supposed to find our worth in God?"

That's what he'd recently learned for himself. "I don't want to fight with you."

She took a deep breath. "I'm sorry for snapping at you that way. Christopher's family. . .let's just say they bent history to suit themselves, and Christopher wanted to erase my lineage altogether to suit the Winstons. Changing it, bending it, ignoring it doesn't change who we are."

"You're right. We are both children of God, and that is what really counts."

She smiled at that.

Good. He'd managed to change the tone back to positive.

&

Rachel sat at the office desk and stared up at her ancestral wall. There were exactly two pieces of paper pinned to the white-papered wall, and she wasn't even sure they belonged. *Grandpa, what were you doing when you gathered all this stuff? Is there any reason to any of it? Am I chasing a rainbow?* So far all her sorting had been a big waste of time. She took a deep breath as she surveyed the room. There had to be one place, one box that her grandpa was collecting all the really important information in. Her pot of gold. But where? Maybe the master bedroom or the dresser in the spare bedroom?

The dresser in the spare room held no surprises. . .and no treasure. Junk and useless papers. She glared at the boxes stacked in the corner. A quick dig in each box should tell her if it was worth further inspection. One by one, the boxes were strewn across the floor along with their contents. Next, the boxes from under the bed. By the time she got to the closet, there was no floor space left; she took those boxes to the living room to disassemble. Nothing. She pulled out the boxes from the top of the closet in the master bedroom and those from under the bed.

She didn't find the end of the rainbow in either room. All she'd gained was a huge mess all over her house. Maybe there was no pot of gold to find.

She went back to the office and sighed. No gold, just a whole lot of boxes, full of nothing. She was tired of this and decided just to give up on the search for today. Her gaze settled on a bookshelf. What had her grandfather enjoyed reading? She knelt in front of it and scanned the selections. There were a few novels, some books about Mackinac Island and Native Americans, and some Bible reference books. On the end of the top shelf was a black leather Bible. She pulled it out. Was her grandfather a Christian? That would be so wonderful to see him in heaven one day and finally get to meet him.

She sat in the desk chair and opened the cover. There was a list of strange names and dates. She turned the page. *To Louise Rogers from Victor and Sarah Rogers, On your 16th Birthday.* This wasn't even her grandfather's Bible. Who was Louise? Or Victor and Sarah?

A knock pulled her from the book. She went to answer the door.

Will held up a flat box. "I brought blueberry pie for dessert. Store-bought, of course."

She blinked at him. Dinner! She jerked up her wrist to look at her watch. "It's that late already? Will, I'm so sorry. I didn't even go to the store. I don't know if I have anything to make a decent meal. I got so wrapped up in things today."

Will's eyes widened at the mess before him. "I see that. Did something happen today?"

"Hmm." She glanced at the mess.

"I thought you had decided to not spread things out so much to organize."

She waved a hand across the living room. "This isn't organized."

"I kind of figured that."

"I was hoping to find one box that my grandpa might have been collecting all the important papers in, because frankly, I don't think anything we've found so far is worth much."

"I didn't think so either but didn't want to say anything. You were so determined to find something. I just can't believe that what we've gone through so far is all Dancing Turtle found. He said he had birth certificates and things that were of more value than what we've seen so far. Did you find a box with everything in it?"

"No. But look at what I did find. What do you make of it?" She handed him the Bible.

He opened the cover. He scanned the list of names and dates. He turned the page. "Who is Louise Rogers? And why did Dancing Turtle have her Bible?"

"I have no clue. I haven't come across the name Louise Rogers before or Victor and Sarah, or any of those names listed in the front."

He turned a couple more pages. Every blank page had names written on it. A smile spread across his face. "This could be good, real good." He fanned the pages to the middle of the Bible. He stopped at a genealogy page. At the top was written *Louise Rogers and Charles Dubois married June 11, 1926.*

Rachel took back the Bible. "My grandfather was married to Louise Rogers? What about Charlotte Coe? I thought she was my grandmother."

"Look at the date. This was before Dancing Turtle was born. Charles and Louise were your grandfather's and Twin Bear's parents."

"My great-grandparents?" She ran her hand down the page of names. Charlotte Coe was listed, Rachel's mother, and there she was. Between Charlotte and Charles was written *not married.* Next to her mother's name, where her father should be, was blank. So no one knew who her father was.

Her mother had taken that information to her grave.

"Can I see what's on the next page?" Will asked.

Will's gentle request pulled her back. She turned the page.

"That's what I thought."

The next page was *FATHER'S FAMILY TREE*. Charles Dubois senior was listed first, then his parents and grandparents and their parents. Three generations back. Seven generations in all. Tears blurred her vision. She could no longer read any of the names. This is where she came from. *Thank you, Great-grandma Louise, for recording all of this.*

"This is the way people used to record, births, deaths, and marriages. Sometimes these were the only records. I'll bet the next page is Louise's family tree. This is what you've been looking for."

She nodded and blinked several times but still couldn't read anything. "It's what I've always wanted." What better place to keep your family than in the Bible. *Thank You, Lord, for helping me find this.*

⁂

Once again, Rachel sat in the desk chair and stared up at her wall of ancestors, but now it actually had something on it. She had spent the day transferring the family information from Great-grandma Louise's Bible to the wall, but it was late and time to head to bed.

One of the sheets of paper, which she'd taped to the ceiling to continue working backwards from Dancing Turtle, drifted to the floor. She had used the last bit of tape to stick that one up. She had found that roll of adhesive tape in the top drawer, the only drawer she'd been in. She shuffled the pens and paper around in that drawer but found no more tape, so she started opening drawers. When she opened the bottom drawer she stopped halfway through closing it. There was no tape, but a file folder had *CHARLOTTE COE* written on it. She held her breath as she took it out along with several others. One said

MY FAMILY, another said *LEWIS'S FAMILY*. Each folder had birth certificates and other documents. This is what she had been looking for. She pulled out a spiral notebook from the same drawer and a leather book.

The leather book was a journal titled *MY SEARCH FOR YOU*. She began skimming the first entry.

> *I know you think that by going away two brothers will mend their relationship, but it was broken before you ever stepped foot on the island.*

She read a few more similar entries and soon realized they were all directed to Charlotte Coe. She flipped past a few pages.

> *You have hidden well.*
> *Where are you?*
> *I'm catching up to you. I searched for evidence that you have given birth to our child. A daughter. Barbara. I like that name. I am praying hard that you don't give her away before I find you.*
> *You are always one step ahead of me.*
> *I wish I could tell you that Lewis and I have put the past to rest, but it has not happened.*
> *You have disappeared, but I have found our daughter, alas it is too late. The paper said she was survived by a daughter. Rachel.*

She choked back a sob at the sight of her name. *He never gave up hope.*

> *I pray still for my brother that if he will not speak to me that he will enter the Lord's family, and we will speak once more in heaven.*

Then the last entry.

Finally, I have found you. And you are so close.

An envelope from a bill was slipped in between that page and the next. An address in St. Ignace was scrawled on it. Whose was it? There was no name.

It had to be her grandma's. *She's alive.* This was too exciting to keep to herself.

sixteen

Ring.

Will startled awake and snatched the phone next to his bed. " 'Lo."

"I hit the jackpot!"

"Rachel?"

"You have to come over right away."

He picked up his bedside clock and moved it around until he could focus on the numbers. "It's not even six." Saturday was his one day a week to sleep in a little.

"Oh, Will, I am so sorry. I wasn't even thinking about the time. You go back to sleep. Come over when you get up." *Click.*

He fumbled to put the phone back into place. Just another hour and he'd be good. *Jackpot.* What had she found? It had to be something good. She sounded really excited. He opened his eyes. He could either lie there for the next hour wondering what she found or just get up. He threw back the covers. *Brr.*

He turned on his coffeepot before jumping into the shower. Once dressed and his thermos full, he headed across the street. When Rachel opened the door, he held up the thermos. "I brought coffee."

She let him in. "I am so sorry for waking you."

"Don't worry about it. I had to get up anyway to answer the phone."

She pulled a face. "Very funny."

"Let me have my first cup of coffee, then you can show me what you found. You want a cup?"

"More than you know."

Those were the same clothes she wore yesterday. "Did you stay up all night or just sleep in your clothes?"

"When I found the 'box' we've been looking for, I got so excited. I just kept sifting through the papers and figuring out where everyone fit."

"Where did you find the box? I thought you opened all of them."

"Follow me." She headed for the office. "I did open every box, but they weren't in a box."

He followed her to the paper strewn office. "Looks like something exploded in here." She just couldn't file papers in a neat orderly way so a person could find them again.

"Don't step on any of them."

It was kind of hard not to. "I'll just stand in the doorway to be safe, and you can fill me in on what happened here." His gaze traveled up the paper covered wall and kept going. "Do you know that you have paper on your ceiling now?"

She tiptoed to the desk. "That wasn't working out once I found the stash. I needed to keep going back and found I wanted to shuffle things around and once they were on the wall it was too hard. So I moved everything to the floor."

"So where did you find all this?" Some of the papers looked like actual birth certificates, others were copies, some printed out info from the computer.

"I was sitting here at the desk looking up at my wall of ancestors, the ones I copied from the Bible, and one of the papers fell off the ceiling. I went searching for more tape. I figured there were just supplies and stuff to take care of bills. That's all I used to have in mine. But this bottom drawer had all this and more." She waved a hand over the room then picked up a handful of file folders. "All these papers were in these files. I think my grandpa had them in some sort of order."

"And you undid that order and tossed them on the floor."

"I didn't toss them, and I numbered each paper on the back lightly in pencil. I can put every one of them back in order. I just had to see everyone all at once."

That made him feel better.

"But the best of all were the two journals." She stood and came over to him in the doorway, holding a spiral notebook. She handed it to him. "This one's for you."

"How do you know?"

"It says so inside."

He opened the front cover. *In the event I am not around to give this to Will Tobin, please see that he receives it.*

He could only stare at Dancing Turtle's words. "What's in here?"

"Well, I confess I flipped through it but didn't really read it. It looks like all the information he gathered he wrote down for you like he promised. I figure if there is anything there that I don't already have, you will let me know."

"I can't believe you didn't actually read this."

"Why? Are you going to be stingy and not share?"

"If you want it, you can keep it. It's your family, and he left everything in the house to you. This was in the house."

"I wouldn't mind making a copy of it just so I have the family's story in his words."

He nodded toward her empty hands. "You said there were two journals."

"The other one is in the living room." She pointed out of the room. "It's the reason I called so early." She picked up a leather journal off the couch and curled her feet under her as she sat. "This one seems to be an accounting of a forty-eight-year quest."

"For what?"

"Not 'for what.' For whom. Charlotte Coe. It's like one long love letter to her. I think he found her before he died." She flipped to the back of the book. " 'Finally, I have found you.

And you are so close.' I think this might be my grandmother's address." She handed him an envelope with an address written on it in pencil.

"There's no name. This could be anybody's."

"But it was tucked in the page where he says he found her."

"Found who? It doesn't say who he found." She was setting herself up again.

"This whole journal is written to Charlotte Coe, just like he wrote that one to you."

"Charlotte Coe could be deceased."

"There was no second date by her name in the Bible to indicate when she died. Why are you being so negative?"

"I don't want to see you hurt again."

"Denying she exists won't change how she feels about me."

He took the envelope to the phone and dialed information.

She came up beside him. "What are you doing?"

"Getting Charlotte's number so you can call her." He gave the operator the information.

"I'm sorry," the brusque voice of the operator came back. "There is no number for that address."

Will gave a heavy sigh as he hung up.

"Did you get it?"

"No. Her number is unlisted." He turned to her. There was only one way for her to talk to Charlotte now. "When do you want to go?"

"Today."

"Bundle up."

She tossed her arms around him. "Thank you."

He was tempted to kiss her right then while she was in his arms, but she just thought he was her friend. *When, Lord?*

She pulled away from him. "I need to take a shower and get ready before we leave."

He stood and grabbed his coat. "I'll come back in about an hour. Will that be enough time?"

"Perfect."

He left and returned an hour later. When she let him in, he handed her the spiral notebook Dancing Turtle had left him. "I read through this while I was waiting. Read the last entry."

" 'I have found my Charlotte at last. I will contact her tomorrow and together we will find our granddaughter.' " She glanced up at him. "That's me," she added before turning back to her reading. " 'I almost have all the information. If Charlotte and I are not able to find her, please find our granddaughter and tell her we love her.' " When she looked up again, tears rimmed her eyes.

"See the date. That's the night he died in his sleep."

"He never got to talk to Charlotte?"

He shook his head.

"That's so sad to look for the one you love your whole life, and then when you find her, you die before you can see her." She wiped a tear that ran down her cheek. "I'm not going to let that happen again."

He handed her a snowsuit. "You can wear this."

seventeen

Will pushed his snowmobile out of his shed. Rachel eyed the machine with about as much enthusiasm as his students on finals' day.

"I'm nervous."

About the snowmobile or seeing Charlotte? He patted the handlebar. "This is perfectly safe." He handed her a helmet with goggles and helped her put it on, adjusting the strap under her chin; then he put on his. He straddled the machine and started it then held a hand out to her.

"I appreciate you doing this." She climbed on behind him.

"No problem. Hold on."

He drove out of town to the beach at British Landing and stopped at the frozen lakeshore. "There it is. The ice bridge. Our link to the outside world."

"What are all the trees for?"

Small evergreens dotted the way across the ice. "They mark the way so we all know where the ice is thickest. Wouldn't want to fall through."

"Is it safe?"

"As long as we stay near the trees."

"How does. . .whoever. . .know where the ice is safe?"

"You can see where the ice starts forming first, and that is generally where it will be thickest. And those that have been on the island for several decades have an instinct about it, I guess."

"Where did all the trees come from?"

"Christmas. The people who have one save it until the bridge freezes. When the ice melts in the spring, they slip quietly into the water. A sort of recycling program. Ready to go?"

"Are you sure it's safe? Maybe we should wait until we can take the plane off the island."

"This is perfectly safe. People have been driving across this for two days."

Just then two snowmobiles pulled up beside them and headed out across the bridge.

"See. People are anxious to get off the island. I don't know if we have ever lost anyone on the ice bridge. No one since I've lived here." He wouldn't tell her that he'd only lived on the island for five years. But that was long enough to hear stories to know the bridge was safe. He also wouldn't tell her about the man three years ago who lost his snowmobile through the ice trying to test if the bridge was solid enough. He'd phoned from St. Ignace to say he was safe but not to let anyone else try to cross. The ice bridge never did freeze solid enough that year to be usable. And this year's bridge didn't look like it would last very long.

"Ready?"

She wrapped her arms around his waist. "Yes."

He pulled down his goggles and drove out onto the firm ice. He liked the feel of her arms around him but couldn't help feeling some measure of guilt. He could have easily borrowed a snowmobile for her to drive herself, but he wanted her close to him, even if they were both bundled up to their eyeballs.

Was it really so wrong to want to be near the woman he loved? Yes, he'd told her he was her friend and he was. He would be her friend until she was ready to be more. Until she could fall in love with him back. He hoped that would be soon.

&

"I told you the ice bridge was safe."

Rachel wasn't sure if she was glad to be on the other side

or not. If she couldn't get off the island, she couldn't see her grandmother. If she couldn't see her grandmother, then there would be no chance of rejection. She should have tried harder to get the number and just called her. Rejection was easier when you didn't have to look the person in the eye, but she physically wanted to see the woman whose features she had inherited.

New fallen snow allowed them to drive all the way to Charlotte Coe's house. When Will came to a stop and cut the engine, she laid the side of her well-covered face against the back of his coat. This was it.

Rachel had encircled Will's waist with her arms, and he put his hand over hers. He gave them a squeeze but didn't move to dismount the snowmobile until she released him.

He took off his helmet and goggles and helped Rachel remove hers; then he pushed down the scarf from around his mouth. "Ready?"

She loosened her scarf as well. "What if she won't see me?"

"What if she will?"

"What if she tells me to go away? I will have no one then."

He cupped her face in his gloved hands. "I can't make you any promises about your grandmother, but I can promise you this: Regardless of how this meeting goes, you will have me, and you will always, always have the Lord. He will never ever leave you. You are part of His family now."

"I know, but with no physical family, I just feel alone. By not meeting her," she pointed toward the house, "I will always have her. If she doesn't want anything to do with me, then I'll have lost her forever."

"You won't know unless you go up to that door and meet her. If she doesn't want to see you, then you start building a new family of Christians, people who will stand beside you no matter what."

But she desperately wanted to have a family of people

related to her. "Would you go up and make sure she still lives here? But don't tell her who I am. I want to do that." She needed a moment alone to gather her courage.

He nodded and walked up the shoveled path.

Lord, give me the strength to accept whatever my grandmother's reaction is. But I really want her to love me.

She could see the front door open, but the screen door remained closed, and Will spoke with the woman who answered. There were several exchanges back and forth before the door closed, and Will came back down the path. "She thinks we are here to swindle her out of her life savings, but it is definitely her."

"You're sure."

He nodded. "She said so. You are going to have to come to the door and tell her who you are."

She walked up the path and rang the bell. The old woman wouldn't come to the door. She rang several more times, but all attempts were ignored. Great. Her grandmother wouldn't see her—not for who she was but for who she thought she was. "What do we do now?"

He shook his head. "I guess we leave and try another day."

She didn't want to leave. She'd had misgivings about coming, but now that she was here, she wanted to meet her grandma. What else could she do but leave? They walked back to the snowmobile as a man, buttoning his coat, came out of the house across the street, heading toward them. "Can I help you?" he called.

She pointed toward the house. "We wanted to see Charlotte Coe, but she won't talk to us."

"Charlotte keeps to herself. What do you want to see her about?"

Should she tell him? She took a deep breath. "I believe I'm her long lost granddaughter."

The man snorted. "Sorry. I just find the *long lost relative* a bit hard to swallow. She's just a lonely old woman living out her days. She doesn't have anything."

"She might have love for me. I want to know if she really is family. That's all I want from her."

He tossed a glance at Will. "And you?"

"Just a supportive friend."

The man turned back to her. "I actually believe you. You have her eyes. I'm Randy Dern." He held his hand out to her. "I'll see if I can get Charlotte to open her door."

She shook his hand and took in a relieved breath. "Thank you." Then she followed him up to the door.

"Charlotte, it's Randy. Open the door." After a moment, a lock clicked as if being unlocked and the door cracked open. "Can we come in?"

"Them two are trying to take all my money."

Rachel's heart went out to the old woman. To be living alone and afraid.

"They just want to talk to you."

Rachel leaned a little forward so her grandmother could see her. "My name is Rachel Coe. My mother's name is Barbara, and I believe she was your daughter."

The door slowly swung open as Charlotte stared at her. "My baby Rachel?"

Charlotte knew her! Tears welled in her eyes, and she nodded.

Her grandmother stared for a moment then fumbled with the lock on the screen door. "I can never get this thing to work when I want it to."

"Lift up on the button on the side," Randy said.

She did so and finally was able to unlock the door. "Well, move out of the way. I can't rightly open the door with you blocking the way."

Randy chuckled at her rebuke. "I'll just be on my way. You have a nice visit." Randy turned to Rachel and said in a low voice, "It will be good for her to have family around."

"Thank you so much."

Rachel and Will stepped inside, and Charlotte closed the door behind them. "Let me take a good look at you."

Rachel unwound her scarf. Will took it from her and then her coat.

Tears filled Charlotte's eyes. "I know you are a grown woman, but would you mind if this old woman gave you a hug?"

Her emotions crashed over her. This woman loved her, even though she didn't know her. "I would like that." A tear slipped down her cheek.

Her grandmother wrapped her thin arms around her, and she hugged the frail woman back. She had family even if it was only one relative.

Her grandmother stepped back from her with tears on her own face. She pulled a tissue out from the cuff of her green cardigan sweater and dabbed at her eyes. "My, how you have grown since the last time."

She wiped her own tear away. She had met her grandmother before? "You've seen me before? I don't remember."

Her grandmother nodded. "In this very house. I'm not surprised you don't remember. You were only eighteen months old. You were here for three days; then Barbara took you away. Never saw you again." Tears rimmed the old woman's eyes. She waved her hand in front of her face as though willing them away. "You would sit in my lap in that rocking chair, and I'd read to you." She pointed to an old wooden rocking chair, then went over to a basket beside the TV and brought back a book. "This was your favorite." She handed her a children's book with a bird on the cover.

Rachel caressed the front of the book. "Why did my mom leave and never come back?"

"Barbara and I'd had a fight as we usually did. She was a

strong-willed one, she was. I came home from work, and the two of you were gone. That is the only time I ever saw you."

She wasn't sure what to call this woman, so she awkwardly used her first name. "Charlotte, do you know who my father is?"

"When you were little, you called me Gumma. I would be honored if you would call me Grandma—but I'll leave that up to you."

"I would like that. . .Grandma." It felt right and natural.

Grandma smiled. "Barbara never did tell me who your father was. Way back when, we had fought, as usual, and she had left, as usual. It was three years before I heard anything from her again. She showed up on my doorstep, out to here with you." She held her hands out in front of her stomach. "No husband. I told her she should have learned something from my mistakes. We fought again, and she left. When she came back again, you were a toddler. I told her the two of you were welcome to stay, but she needed to get a job to help out. The next thing I knew, she was gone. And you with her."

So it was her mother's choice not to keep in touch with family. *Why, Mom? I could have grown up knowing my family instead of being alone.*

Grandma blinked several times. "Where are my manners? I never offered you anything to drink. I have orange juice in the refrigerator. Coffee or tea. It will only take a jiffy to heat water in the tea kettle."

"Tea would be nice."

Grandma looked at Will, whom they had both been ignoring. "And you?"

"Tea will be fine."

Her grandma left, and Rachel turned to Will. "I'm sorry for ignoring you. I got so caught up in finally meeting her."

"Don't worry about it. You should take every moment you can to get to know her. You are finally getting the family you wanted. I'm enjoying watching the two of you."

"You really don't mind?"

"Not at all. I'm merely an observer."

When Grandma came back with mugs of tea, she handed one to each of them and sat in the rocking chair. The rocking chair her grandma had read to her in. Grandma turned her attention to Will. "My bad manners seem to be coming out all over the place. I didn't even let my granddaughter introduce you."

"I'm Will Tobin."

"I don't see a ring on either of your fingers."

"I'm just a friend. I gave Rachel a ride over the ice bridge from Mackinac Island on my snowmobile."

"It's nice to have good friends you can depend on."

Will was certainly a good friend, but she thought of him as something more. But what?

Suddenly, her grandma stood. "Oh here, let me show you something." She left and returned with an old shoebox. She sat on the couch next to her and slowly removed the lid. The box was full of old photographs. She started digging and pulled out a picture of a dark-haired toddler holding a pink kitty, grinning so hard her nose was crinkled up. "This is my favorite picture of you."

Rachel took the picture. "This is me?"

"When you squeezed the paw it would meow. It would make you laugh every time."

"I remember that cat. I don't remember it ever meowing. The batteries probably ran out, and Mom never replaced them."

"How is Barbara?"

"Mom passed away seven years ago. Cancer."

Her grandma shifted the box to her lap and got up, leaving the room. Rachel watched her leave, and her own ache at losing her mom welled up inside her again. She hadn't been a great mom, but she was the only one she had. And Mom had loved her.

Will scooted next to her. "She probably needs time to adjust to such sad news."

"That news is never easy to take. Or to give." She sifted through the pictures; several more of her as a toddler, her mom's high-school pictures, and others of people she didn't know.

After a while, her grandma returned and sat back down. She took out each picture and told who was in each. She came to one of twin black-haired boys about nine years old. "This is the only picture I have of your grandfather. He's the one on the left."

Her heart beat faster. But who was the one on the right? Charles or Lewis? She was almost afraid to ask. She wanted so much to be Charles's granddaughter. He had wanted her, searched for her. She pointed to the boys in the picture from left to right. "Charles and Lewis?"

"Yes. I was several years younger than them. Lewis used to tease me, and serious Charles would always come to my rescue. I really loved them both."

"But Charles is my grandfather?"

"Yes."

She gave a mental sigh. What a relief. What little she had been allowed to know about Lewis's side of the family had not been that great. She would much rather be the granddaughter of the brother who might have actually wanted her. "What happened? Why didn't you and Grandpa ever marry?"

"Lewis used to always say he was going to marry me. I never took him seriously. And I never fell in love with him. Charles was my champion. We pledged our love to each other under the stars before God. We somehow thought that would make what we were about to do all right. It didn't, and I became pregnant. Charles wanted to marry me, but I saw the wedge it was driving between the two brothers. So I left. I knew if I left I could never come back. I knew it would take time for their relationship to heal. I would give them a lifetime if that was what it took."

Even a lifetime hadn't been enough. She felt so bad. Grandma had given up a life with the man she loved so that Charles and Lewis wouldn't have a breech between them. She didn't have the heart to tell her that her sacrifice had been in vain.

Will looked at his watch. "We need to be going. We don't want to risk being out on the ice after dark."

When she stood to leave, Grandma grabbed her hand and squeezed it. "You will come back, won't you?"

Grandma looked as afraid as she was to lose what little family she had. "I promise, and you have my phone number on the island."

"I don't have service. Call Randy's; he'll let me know you made it." Grandma turned to Will. "You take good care of my little Rachel."

He smiled. "I will."

eighteen

Tomorrow night she would make dinner for Will. Maybe their relationship would start moving forward. She was tired of just being his friend and his regular comments about him coming over to see her—just as a friend—and how it was nice for them to be friends. He wanted more, and now she felt she was ready for more. But there was something that was bothering her. She would take care of it first, then she'd stop by the store to get a couple of things she needed for tomorrow night's meal.

The sleigh taxi stopped in front of the library. She paid the driver and got out, keeping one hand securely in her pocket. One of the horses shook his head, jingling his harness. She stepped inside and up to the circulation desk. "Is the head librarian here?"

"I'm the head librarian." A svelte woman in her forties came over by the desk where Rachel stood. It was the same woman who'd directed her to the school in the fall. "How may I help you?"

"How would I go about making a donation to the library?"

The librarian's smile widened. "Make a check payable to the library, and I'll see the right person gets it."

"What if it isn't a check?"

"I can write you out a receipt."

"Is there someplace private we can do this? I want my donation to be anonymous."

"Of course."

She followed the woman through a door in the back of the library. "This is where we repair books, do cataloging, a catchall room, and sometimes the lunchroom. We call it our everything room. Have a seat." She pointed to one of the four chairs around a wooden table.

She pulled a handkerchief out of her coat pocket and laid it on the table. Then she pulled back the corners to reveal the jewelry Christopher had given her.

The woman sucked in a breath. "Are you sure about this?"

Christopher had said he didn't want them back. Well, she didn't want them either. They were a reminder of a life she shouldn't have strived for. They were holding her back. Holding her to a man she would never marry. She wanted to be free of them, and what better way than to donate the jewelry gifts to a good cause. She could have sold them and used the money for something else, but that didn't feel right. She just wanted to be done with them. Not to have to hassle with trying to find somewhere to sell them. Let the library worry about that. "Positive. These are all the real deal. Don't let anyone try to cheat you out of their worth."

She picked up the ruby necklace. "Why would you want to get rid of these?"

"My ex-fiancé gave them to me. I have no need for them."

"Won't he want them back?"

"He wouldn't take them. They are the library's—free and clear."

≈

After the last bell of the day rang, Will went down to the office to check his teacher box for any messages or flyers. Most of the staff and a fist full of parents were gathered, clucking like hens.

"Can you believe that? They think they are worth several thousand dollars."

"The ring alone could be worth at least a couple Gs."

He tapped a fellow teacher on the shoulder. "What's going on? What are they talking about?"

Karen turned to him. "Someone donated a bunch of jewelry to the library."

"Who?"

"No one knows. A good-looking brunette. There was a ruby necklace and earrings, diamond tennis bracelet, and a very expensive diamond engagement ring."

Rachel? She gave away her engagement ring?

Maybe she was ready to move on. *Is this my great big clue, Lord? Is this Your way of telling me it's okay to move beyond friendship?* He gave a soft snort. His heart had moved beyond friendship a long time ago. Her act of generosity also told him money wasn't a central focus in her life. That was important, because as a teacher he would never make a lot of money.

He couldn't wait to get over to her house to confirm his suspicions.

* * *

"You know how to create quite a stir."

Rachel pulled her eyebrows together in confusion. "And what is that supposed to mean?"

"Giving your engagement ring and other expensive jewelry to the public library."

Her eyes widened. "That was supposed to be anonymous."

Yes! It was you.

"The librarian promised," she said.

"As far as I know, your secret is safe. Only you, the librarian, and I know."

"Who told you?"

He scrubbed his hand across his mouth reluctant to admit it. "You just did."

"What?"

"By what everyone was saying, I guessed it was you."

"What were people saying?" She looked horrified that people were talking about her.

She didn't have anything to worry about. How could

anyone say anything bad about her? "Just that a beautiful brunette donated several thousand dollars worth of jewelry. . . including a large diamond engagement ring. It didn't take a genius to figure it out. There aren't too many people on the island who fit that profile. Someone is eventually going to recognize you; then the cat will be out of the bag."

"I can always deny it. Plead the fifth."

"The scuttle is that they are stolen."

"I did not steal them. Christopher gave me that jewelry. I tried to give it back, but he wouldn't take it. What else was I supposed to do with it?"

That was good to know that she didn't want to keep gifts from her ex. Giving it away told him she had severed her emotional ties to her ex, and she wasn't interested in the money or she would have sold them and kept the money. But that question was a good one. "Why didn't you sell the jewelry and keep the money?"

"That just didn't feel right. I didn't feel like I had the right to keep them since I wouldn't be marrying him. And since he wouldn't take them back, I thought that donating them to a good cause would be the perfect solution. They don't mean anything to me except that I wasn't good enough because I have Native American blood in my veins."

She was definitely good enough.

"Would you tell them that none of that jewelry was stolen?"

He shook his head. "No need. They'll figure it out. If I speak up, they may find you more easily. If you really want your donation to be anonymous, it's best if we both stay out of it."

❧

Rachel had just finished chopping the vegetables for the stir-fry and had everything else prepped and ready to throw into the pan when the knock sounded on her door. That would be Will.

She opened the door. Will stood outside with his hands braced on either side of the door. He didn't make a move to enter.

"You want to come in?"

"That depends."

This behavior was odd. "On what?"

"On whether or not I'm welcome."

"I have welcomed you every other time you've come over, why not today?"

"Because I'm not here as just a friend today."

"Oh." She felt a gentle smile pull at her mouth. "You're still welcome."

He didn't budge. "One more thing. If I step across this threshold, I'm planning on kissing you before I step back across it."

Her insides twisted at that declaration. She opened the door wider and waved him in.

"I just didn't want there to be any misunderstandings."

Her insides twisted more in anticipation of his promise as she closed the door. She wasn't anxious for him to leave, but she knew she wouldn't be able to concentrate on anything else until he did. "Just get it over with." She bit her bottom lip.

He raised his eyebrows to her. "Get what over with?"

"The kiss."

He removed his coat and hung it on the coat tree. "Well, put like that, it doesn't sound very appealing."

"I didn't mean it like that. I just know I won't be able to think about anything else until I know what it is like to have you kiss me. I have been wondering for some time."

"You have?"

She nodded.

"I wasn't planning on kissing you until later."

"Well, I'm not going to beg."

He stepped closer and put one arm around her waist. "This

kiss doesn't count as the one I promised." He caressed a lock of hair away from her face. "I still reserve the right to kiss you later as well."

She barely managed a nod.

He leaned into her and brushed his lips against hers.

It was every bit as wonderful as she had thought it would be.

He pulled away. His voice was husky. "Happy now?"

She took a deep breath and opened her eyes. "Mm-hmm."

"I've waited a long time to do that."

"Wait here. I have something for you." She went to her bedroom and grabbed the handles of the gift bag Will had given her before Christmas. She held it out to him.

He didn't take it. "You're giving back my gift?"

"I'm just recycling the bag. I couldn't find any wrapping paper around here."

He nodded and took the bag. "What's the occasion?"

"You can just call it a belated or early birthday present, whichever fits."

"Birthday, huh?"

"You have a birthday sometime every year. Or call it a thank-you gift, or a very late Christmas present. Take your pick. Go ahead and open it."

He set the bag on the dining table and pulled out the blue tissue paper wrapped around the trifold picture frame, a center five-by-seven flanked by four two-by-threes. He stared at the photos of her wearing the iridescent white dress. They were what Mark had called his Cinderella photos. Some of the pictures were taken with her wearing a pair of feather wings.

The five-by-seven was her favorite. She had on the wings and was taking a break while the next shot was being set up. Mitzy had draped a white cloth over a large rock for her to sit on. She had bowed her head to pray and wasn't even aware that the sun had broken through the gray sky to cast a ray of light on a small white flower poking out of the ground in front of her. The glitter Mitzy had applied to her face made it look like she glowed. Mark had snapped several shots before she'd noticed and the light faded.

"Those were taken the last day of the Europe shoot."

"These are incredible."

nineteen

The next weekend, Will picked her up right after school on Friday and whisked her across the ice bridge before dark to stay at her grandma's house for the weekend. He would visit his mother while he was on the mainland.

"Have a good visit. I'll come back Sunday morning and take you to church before we head back to the island." He gave her a kiss before getting into the passenger side of his mom's car.

His mom leaned over to look out his window. "It was nice meeting you."

"It was nice meeting you, too."

He stretched his hand out the window and took hers. "I'll miss you."

"I'll miss you, too." She watched the car pull away in the dark with the snowmobile on a trailer behind. She looked forward to Sunday.

When she entered the house, Grandma moved away from the window. "He's a nice man. I like him."

"Me, too." She went over to her backpack she'd crammed in the things she could bring for the weekend. "I brought you something." She handed her grandma the leather journal. "Grandpa wrote this to you."

Grandma took it and caressed the cover. "Thank you."

"It's his quest to find you."

Grandma hugged it to herself. "You don't mind if I turn in now and read for a bit?"

"Go right ahead." She'd expected as much.

The next morning, the neighbor came over.

"Would you like some coffee?" Grandma asked Randy.

"I would love some." When Grandma reached the kitchen, Randy said, "Are you really her granddaughter?"

"Yes."

He lowered his voice to a whisper. "Then you ought to know that her social security checks don't cover all her bills."

"Really? How has she been making it?"

"Last summer they shut off her electricity. She couldn't pay it."

"What?"

"I tried to talk her into moving into a place she could afford, but she refused. She said if her daughter came back, it would be to this house."

"But she has electricity now."

"I told the electric company to send her bill to me. My wife brings over some of our leftovers in small containers and puts them in the refrigerator. We're afraid she might not always be eating well."

"Do you know how much she owes on this house?" Maybe she could pay it off.

"Nothing. I do."

"You own this house?"

He turned to Charlotte as she came back into the room and took the mug from her, ending the conversation. "Thank you."

This conversation may be over for now, but she needed to know more.

Later, after Randy left, she said, "I'm going to go for a walk. Do you want to come?"

"No, thank you, darling. I don't want to slip on the ice. Old bones don't heal so easily."

She didn't expect her grandma would want to go out in the cold. It would give her a chance to talk more with Randy about her grandma's situation. She knocked on the door. Randy invited her in. "Would you like some coffee?"

"No, thank you. Does my grandma know you are paying some of her bills?"

"She thinks God is miraculously providing. God may be providing through my wife and me, but I don't think it could count as a miracle. We don't want to kick her out. She's a sweet old lady, but we can't keep losing money."

"I wouldn't expect you to. I have a small house on Mackinac Island. I'll talk her in to moving there with me. I don't know how easy it will be to move in the winter."

"We've been praying for some kind of solution, and it looks like you may be it. You don't have to be in a big rush. You can store some of her things in the garage until you can get them in the spring."

"Thank you. That would be very helpful." An excitement bubbled up from deep inside her. She not only found her grandma who loved her, but her grandma would be coming to live with her. You couldn't have family any closer than living in your own house. She hoped that would be all right with her grandma. Hopefully she wasn't too attached to the house and refused to move, but if she was only there, as Randy said, so that Barbara could find her, then she shouldn't have any objections.

&

Will stepped inside Charlotte Coe's house. He'd come earlier than planned because he missed Rachel. He was taking her to church. She stood before him with her bottom lip captured between her teeth. "What's wrong?"

She opened her mouth to speak then closed it then opened it again. "My grandma doesn't own this house and can't really afford to live here, so I invited her to come live with me."

"So?"

"She wants to go today. She's almost all packed. All three of us and her belongings can't fit on your snowmobile and the trailer sled. I don't know how to tell her she can't go today. We spent half the night packing, and then she got up early and was at it again. And what about getting groceries? That is why you brought the sled after all."

He looked to the boxes and suitcases piled in the living room and scrubbed his hand over his mouth. "Is this all there is?"

"Pretty much. I think she is filling one more small suitcase." She pulled her lip back in between her teeth.

"What about the furniture?"

"It stays with the house except the rocking chair."

How long would it take to get some groceries, take them over to the island and come back for two or three trips, maybe four? There wasn't enough daylight to do it all. How did he tell her it was impossible? He turned back to her and looked into her pleading hazel eyes. "Where's the phone?"

"She doesn't have one, but Randy, across the street, will let you use his."

"I'll be right back." Once at the neighbor's, he dialed the phone. "Hey, Garth. You busy?"

"I was just about to leave for church. The kids are sick, so Lori's staying home with them."

"Remember when you moved to the island you said you owed me one or twelve. When you get back from church, would you mind bringing your snowmobile across the bridge with your trailer sled?"

"What's up?"

He filled Garth in on what he was trying to do.

"I'll be there right after the service."

"I appreciate that."

He walked back to Charlotte's. There was no way to get even half her stuff on two snowmobiles not to mention the groceries both he and Rachel were planning on buying. He was out of practically everything.

He took Rachel to church, then to the grocery store. As he loaded their food on the sled, he said, "It will be impossible to get all her things over to the island before dark. Maybe two trips with both Garth and my machines. I can take tomorrow off work and make whatever trips are needed to get the rest."

"Oh, Will. I don't know what to say. That is so nice of you. I hate to have you take time off work."

"I'm glad to do it."

"Why would you do this for a woman you hardly know?"

He cupped her face in his hands. "Because I love you."

Her eyes widened.

She hadn't expected him to say that. He hadn't expected it either, but it had been true for a long time, and she might as well know it. "Don't feel like you have to say it back. Two people don't always fall in love at the same pace."

Tears rimmed her eyes.

He leaned in and kissed her, then wiped away a stray tear. "Let's go prioritize your grandma's things so we know what she wants to go today and what can wait until tomorrow."

❧

Rachel stood in the doorway to her grandma's kitchen and watched Will help an old woman sort through the pile of boxes and suitcases. He was patiently explaining that it all couldn't go today. He'd done all he could to ensure her grandma and some of her belongings could go.

She still wasn't sure what to think about him saying he loved her. They'd only been dating a week, so he'd probably been in love before that. Now looking back she could see that he did. All the while he was being her friend, he had been patiently loving her as well. Did she love him, too? What was love? How would she know?

The rumble of a snowmobile outside drew her attention, and she went to the window.

"That should be Garth," Will said.

Garth pulled up at the front of the pack of half a dozen snowmobiles with trailers. "And the snowmobile brigade."

Will set down a large suitcase and came to the window, then went out the front door. She followed him.

Garth saluted them. "Your Mackinac Island moving team."

Rachel folded her arms across her front to ward off the cold. "You brought all these people to help move?"

"At your service." Garth bowed.

She couldn't believe it. "This is amazing."

"Lori called a few of our students while I was at church. I asked Don at church. We picked up Troy on the way. He wanted to join the parade."

Seven more snowmobiles without sleds roared up the street. Garth thumbed toward the latest arrivals. "The news traveled pretty fast through the student body. I think they just wanted an excuse to get off the island."

twenty

It was a few weeks later when Will squeezed her hand as they stepped off the ferry. "Don't worry, my mom will love you."

Surprisingly, she wasn't worried. She had agreed to spend the weekend with his family. She had met Will's mom briefly the day she picked him up at her grandma's. "You have three sisters, right?" He nodded. "What are their names and ages again?" It was important to know people's names. It helped make them feel comfortable.

"Mandy is almost twenty-three and married. She lives in Plymouth near Detroit with her husband Jake. Bethany is eighteen, a senior in high school but is on a church retreat this weekend or something. Lauren is the baby. She's fifteen and a freshman in high school. She's the only one who will be there today besides Mom."

That would make it easier. "And your mom's name is Linda." He nodded. All she had to do was remember Linda and Lauren. Things seemed to be moving quickly now that they had started dating.

Will's mom met them at the ferry. "It is so good to see you again."

She shook Linda's outstretched hand.

After they got into the car, Linda said, "I must apologize. Will's sister Mandy and her husband came up from Plymouth last night. She couldn't stand not to meet you. And Bethany was sick yesterday and stayed home from school, so she wasn't able to go on the youth group retreat. Don't worry. She isn't all that sick. I think she didn't want to be the only one not meeting you. I know Will told you it was only going to be Lauren and me, so don't blame him; he had no knowledge of them all scheming to be here. I made them promise to not interrogate you."

She was used to meeting new people. How would a houseful of girls be that different from a dressing room full of models? Probably a lot easier. And saner.

Once at the house, everyone introduced themselves but didn't crowd her. She met Mandy's husband, Jake. They'd been married a year. Everyone was making an effort to be polite and not pelt her with questions, which made the room unnaturally quiet and the climate awkward.

Will had gone outside with Jake to replace a burned out headlight on his SUV. Linda had run to the store to get salad dressing, butter, and ice cream.

So Rachel stood in the kitchen with Will's two youngest sisters cutting vegetables for the salad while Mandy stood watch over the fried chicken and fried potatoes. "I know your mom told you not to interrogate me, but there is nothing wrong with asking a few questions. You do have questions, don't you?"

They each acknowledged her with either a nod or a smile, but no one was brave enough to ask a question.

Well, no one told her she couldn't interrogate them. "So, Bethany, Will tells me that you are in the drama club."

Bethany gave her a shy smile and nodded.

"What play are you doing?"

"*Guys and Dolls.*"

"What part do you have?"

"Sarah."

"Isn't that one of the leads?"

She nodded.

Getting her to talk was like pulling teeth. Maybe she'd have better luck with Lauren. "What is your favorite thing about school?"

Lauren gave a sly smile. "You mean anything? Not like a class?"

She nodded.

"Eric Buchanan. He is so hot. He sits in the lunchroom strumming on his acoustic guitar. Sometimes he'll sing these songs that he wrote."

"There are only a couple he actually wrote." Bethany kept her head down as she spoke.

"You're a freshman, right, Lauren? What grade is Eric in?"

"He's a senior." Lauren gave her sister a sideways glance. "Bethany has a crush on him."

"I do not!"

Lauren mouthed, "She does so."

Suddenly a chunk of carrot flew across the kitchen island and hit Lauren in the shoulder. Lauren turned to her sister. "Then how come wherever Eric is, you are?"

"None of your business." Bethany glared at her little sister.

Maybe a subject change would be in order. "Lauren, if you could ask me any question what would it be?"

"Mom said not to."

"I said *if you could*?"

Lauren's mouth stretched into a wide grin. "What is it like to be a model? Do you travel all over the world? Will said you were in Europe. What was it like? Did you go to Paris?"

That broke the dam. She answered all Lauren's questions and more as well as questions from Mandy. Bethany even ventured a question or two.

Later, after Rachel changed for bed, she looked around Will's old room. Will was sleeping on the couch in the living room, and everyone else had done some room swapping to make a place for everyone. On Will's old dresser sat five model cars that he'd probably built, a baseball and glove, a baseball trophy, and a framed photo of a Brittany spaniel.

Nothing to be jealous of there. No photos of old girlfriends anywhere.

A knock on the door drew her from Will's memorabilia. Who could that be? Rachel cracked the door a little and saw Bethany standing in the hall. She opened the door wider and invited her in; then she closed the door so as not to disturb anyone else. "What can I do for you?"

Bethany just shrugged.

"You obviously came for a reason. Did you need something?"

"No—well, sort of. Not really."

She sat on the edge of the bed and patted it, inviting Bethany to join her. "What is it?"

Bethany hesitated a moment then sat. "Do you love my brother?"

There was a question no one had asked her yet, and one she'd been trying to figure out the answer to since Will told her he loved her three weeks ago. "Yes, I think I do."

"How do you know when you love somebody? I mean how do you know it's not just a crush?"

Not how did she know she loved Will but a generic somebody. "I don't quite know how to answer that. I guess I know I love your brother because I like being around him. When I'm not, I miss him." A smile pulled at her mouth. "I think about him when I'm not around him when I'm doing other things. He's always there in my thoughts."

Bethany nodded.

She sensed there was something more to Bethany's question than just finding out if his brother's girlfriend was in love with him. "Are you asking because you really do like Eric?"

Bethany dipped her head as she shook it. "His best friend. Don't tell Lauren."

"I won't. I don't even know his name, and as long as I don't,

I can't slip. Does he like you, too?"

"I don't know. He probably doesn't even know who I am."

That was so sad to like someone who had no clue, and Bethany was too shy to drop this boy any clues. She, herself, had been clueless about Will's attraction to her. She found it silly now that, back then, she thought he was only being neighborly. Now that she knew him better, it was so obvious; the little looks he'd give her, the way he would help her. Yes, she loved him. . . . But was love enough?

⁑

Will put his arm around Rachel's shoulders as the ferry raced back toward Mackinac Island on Sunday. "My family loved you. Lauren was really taken by you. She wants to be a model."

"I liked them all, too."

He squeezed her shoulder. "You seem different today. Happier maybe. Almost mysterious or impish—like you have a secret." He couldn't put his finger on it. It wasn't anything overt. Nothing specific. It was like it was her whole demeanor, her outlook.

"Maybe I do. Bethany came to my room last night."

He guessed she didn't want to talk about what the change was he'd seen in her. "I thought I heard people creeping around upstairs. What did she want?"

"What she wanted to know and what she asked were only mildly related. She wanted to know how you know when you're in love."

"What did you tell her?"

"Basically that the other person occupies all your thoughts."

"Then I must truly be in love because you are always on my mind." He kissed the side of her head.

"When she came in the room, you know what she asked?"

"Since I wasn't there, I don't see how I could."

"She asked me if I loved her brother."

His heart skipped a beat, and he held his breath for a moment. "Two people don't fall in love at the same time. It's okay if you don't feel as strongly for me yet."

"I know."

"What did you tell her?" He held his breath again.

"That I love you."

He let out his captive breath and wrapped both arms around her. "I love you, too." He kissed her for a long time. Then she rested her head on his shoulder. This is exactly where he wanted her. At his side.

"I'm afraid."

"Afraid of what?"

"Of it all ending. Of losing you."

"You're not going to lose me."

"I hope not."

He didn't want to lose her either. *Lord, help her feel secure in my love for her.*

৯

Winter faded into spring and the island lilac bushes were loading their branches with new leaves and bunches of tight little buds preparing to bloom in a week or so. By the middle of June, the whole island would smell fresh and sweet. Tourists were already beginning to swarm the area.

Rachel turned over the envelope, hand-addressed: *RACHEL COE (& WILL)*. The envelope paper was heavy invitation-weight stock. She slid her finger under the flap, not even caring what someone like Christopher would say.

It was an invitation to Hayden's graduation.

The short letter enclosed on notebook paper read:

> *I know my family is a bunch of pinheads, but I'd like to have you there. There is a graduation celebration party for all the graduates and their families at Bayfront Park. You and Will are welcome to come.*

Hayden may welcome her, but the rest of the family wouldn't. Whether they wanted to acknowledge her or not, they had to realize she wasn't going away simply because they wanted her to.

ã‚

As soon Rachel saw Will come up the street, she trotted across the street and waited for him to park his bike in his shed.

When he came out of the shed and saw her, he smiled. "Hello. I like this kind of greeting when I come home."

"Hayden has invited both of us to his graduation. Will you go with me?" She hoped he would, but his smile slipped to a frown.

Will looked at her a moment working his jaw back and forth. "Why do you want to do that to yourself?"

"Do what?"

"Set yourself up for rejection. You know the rest of the family is going to be there, and they won't want you there."

"I'm not going to reject Hayden just because the rest of the family rejects me. He's still family."

"You being there will only make the whole event awkward and strained."

"He wants me there."

"So he can make his family mad."

She knew that was probably the case. Regardless of his motives, he was still family and had invited her. "Do you want to come with me or not?"

"I'm not going to let you walk into a lions' den. I can't just stand by and watch them treat you like a rabid dog. It tears me up inside just thinking about the anguish they will cause you. You can always call him and tell him you won't be able to make it. Wish him well and send a card."

Oh, how she had wished there had been family for her when she graduated. All she had was a terminally ill mom who was in her last couple of months of the fight for her life. . .and losing. She would trade her graduation experience for all the strife Twin Bear's family could dish out. It was nothing compared to the strife of your only family member dying.

"I just can't go and watch you be hurt. I don't think I could handle that. When they rejected you before, it made me so mad I wanted to hit someone or grab that old man by the shirt and tell him what an idiot he was for pushing you away. I may do something rash."

That made her feel good to know he wanted to protect her from hurt, but it also hurt that he didn't feel like he could be there for her. "I'm disappointed, but I understand."

Later that evening, she called Hayden. "I'm coming to your graduation."

"Really? Cool. I thought maybe you'd have some excuse because of the bozos I'm related to."

"Graduation is an important milestone. I want to be there for you."

"Is Will coming?"

"I'm afraid not."

"Bummer. He seemed like a cool guy."

She didn't want to get into why he wasn't coming. "I'm going to need really good directions."

"No problem."

&

"I've changed my mind." Will wanted to be there for her. He wouldn't abandon her like Twin Bear's family had. "I'll go to Hayden's graduation with you."

She grabbed him around the neck and hugged him. "Thank you. You don't know how much this means to me."

He would do just about anything for her, including using self-restraint if Twin Bear's family was cruel to her. He'd just escort her out and console her. "Any day but Saturday."

She pushed away from him. "But it is this Saturday."

He shook his head. "What time? Maybe I can make both."

"It's sort of an all-day event. Make both what?"

"Bethany's graduation is Saturday. Where is Hayden's? Is it in Cheboygan?"

"No. Let me get the directions he gave me." She handed him the paper she'd scrolled them on.

"Petoskey High School?" He looked up from the paper. This was incredible. "He's graduating from Petoskey? That's where I'm from. There's only one high school. That means Hayden and Bethany are classmates. They'll be graduating together."

She smiled. "I guess it's true what they say, 'It's a small world after all.'"

Maybe a little too small.

Later that evening, Will called his sister. "Bethany, I was wondering if you could tell me a little something about one of your classmates. Do you know Hayden Dubois?"

Silence.

"Beth?"

"Yeah, I know him sort of. Why?"

"What kind of kid is he?"

"Has Rachel been talking to you?"

"What?" Why was she changing the subject? "I just want to know if he's a troublemaker."

A pause. "No. . .he's not a troublemaker."

Why were his sister's answers guarded?

"Why do you want to know about Hayden?"

"He is Rachel's second cousin. He invited her to graduation, and I just found out that he goes to your school. I thought you might know him. I just wanted to know more about him. He wouldn't purposely do anything to hurt her, would he?"

"No. He does goofy stuff but nothing mean," she said.

"What kind of stuff?"

"Him and another boy stood on the tables in the cafeteria and sang 'Chestnuts' the day before Christmas break started.

They bought ten windup alarm clocks and set them to go off at different times and put them behind the books in the library. Just goofy stuff like that."

Knowing how the librarians liked the silence, that probably set them on edge not knowing when and where the next one would go off. He was relieved to know that Hayden was only mischievous and not mean.

൞

After the graduation ceremony, people mingled on the grass, waiting for the food to be served. Rachel stood to the side with Will's family. She turned to Bethany. "My cousin Hayden also graduated. Do you know him or where I might find him?" She wanted to congratulate him and give him his gift.

"Will told me he was your cousin. I saw him over there. I'll show you."

"Will, I'm going to go find Hayden."

"I'll come with you." He laced his finger with hers.

She was glad he was coming. She liked having him at her side. It was comfortable and felt right.

Bethany led the way.

Will leaned closer to her. "I asked her about him. I wanted to know if he was the kind of kid who might be setting you up. I just wanted to go into today with my eyes open. No surprises. I hope you don't mind."

It was nice to have someone looking out for her. She'd never really had that. "It's fine."

Hayden was in a cluster of kids. In the center to be exact, standing on a table with another boy who had a guitar. That must be Eric. The two boys were belting out a 70s rock song about school being out. The students around them were dancing and singing along. They really had the crowd going. When she glanced over at Bethany, Bethany was gazing up at the two boys, drew in a deep breath, and sighed softly. If

Bethany's crush wasn't on Eric, then it had to be Hayden. Did he know?

After the song was over and the crowd loosened up, Rachel caught Hayden's gaze. As he strode over to her, Bethany's head slowly lowered. Yes, Hayden was definitely the object of Bethany's affections. Did he even have a clue?

"Hey, Cuz. I'm glad you made it." Hayden turned to Will. "Rachel said you weren't going to make it. I'm glad you did."

Will stretched out his hand and shook Hayden's. "It turned out that my sister was graduating from the same high school."

Hayden turned to Bethany. "Bethany, right? You sit up front by the teacher."

At least he knew who she was, even if he didn't look interested in her.

The red in Bethany's face deepened. She nodded. "I don't like to miss anything."

To rescue Bethany from any further torture, Rachel held out Hayden's gift to him. "This is from my grandma Charlotte and me."

"Charlotte Coe? You found her? Cool. You should have brought her."

"We didn't see how any good could come out of her being here. There would only be more hurt feelings."

"That's true."

ॐ

Rachel had seen Hayden's family across the crowd during the ceremony, including Twin Bear. Now Twin Bear sat alone in the shade in a lawn chair. This was her chance. She touched Will's arm. "I'm going to go talk to him."

"I'll come with you."

"Thanks, but I need to do this alone."

Twin Bear watched her approach and made eye contact, but when she got closer he looked away.

She stood beside him for a moment not quite sure what to say. "Hi. It's me, Rachel."

He remained quiet for a moment. "I drove her away. Drove you away. I even drove my own brother away. I drove them all away."

She gripped the arm of his chair for balance and squatted down next to him. "You haven't driven me away. I'm still here."

A tear rolled down his cheek as he turned toward her but didn't look her in the face. Instead he covered her hand with his.

"Your brother always wanted to mend your relationship. He wanted to tell you about God's love for you so you would go to heaven."

"Charlotte taught me about that."

She somehow knew he wasn't talking about his daughter.

"If I accept God"—he looked her square in the eyes—"then I'd have to forgive her for not loving me."

How sad to know about the love God has for him but not accept it because you are mad at someone. "It's time to let it go. Let her go."

He patted her hand then took his away. "It's too late for me. Everyone hates me."

She knelt in front of him and took both his hands in hers. "It's never too late. Your family is scattered and broken, but you can show them God's love if you'll only accept Him."

He looked out across the park. "They would never listen to me. I've hurt them all too much."

"When they see the change in you, they'll listen."

He looked at her. "You're sure an optimistic dreamer."

"I'm learning that God can do incredible things. So what do you say?"

"I'll think on it."

She guessed that was progress. "I'll be praying that you do more than think on it."

He looked above her then and pulled his hands away. "He's not going to hit me, is he?"

She glanced back and saw Will standing near. She smiled and shook her head. "No, he won't hit you." Though his scowl was intimidating. She stood and brought Will closer. She squeezed his hand. "You're frowning." She turned to Twin Bear. "This is my boyfriend, Will Tobin."

twenty-one

Later that night, Will sat on his couch with Rachel nestled up next to him. Wavering candles provided the only light; soft music played on his stereo. It was late and had been a long day. He should be walking her home, but he didn't want to let her go just yet.

Rachel shifted slightly. "It turned out to be a great day."

"Yes, it did."

"You didn't have to come back to the island with me. You could have stayed with your family."

"Though I love my family, I'd much rather be here with you. My family has figured out that they are losing out to you."

She turned and faced him. "I like being here with you, too. It's the perfect ending to the perfect day."

He hugged her. Nearly perfect. There was one thing that could make it better. And this felt like the perfect time. He kissed the top of her head and pulled his arm out from around her. "I'll be right back."

"Where are you going?"

"To truly make this a perfect day. Don't move." He went to his room and got his mom's rings out of his drawer. "Close your eyes." He put the wedding band back. He didn't need that one yet. "Are they closed?"

"Yes."

He came out and knelt before her, holding out the ring. "Okay. Open them."

She sucked in a breath.

"Rachel, will you marry me?"

"It's beautiful."

"Is that a yes?"

"Oh, Will. I want to say yes, but I don't know if I can."

"Why not? You just have to say yes." It was simple in his mind.

"I don't know if I'm ready to make that kind of commitment."

"We can have a long engagement if you like."

She took his arms. "Here. Sit back on the couch." When he did, she continued. "I don't know if I'll ever be ready. My mom didn't do so well when she married. I don't want to be like that. I want it once forever."

"That's what I want, too." He wouldn't even consider marriage if he thought it wouldn't last a lifetime. "I want to grow old with you."

"I'm just not sure."

"You were going to get married before. Were you sure then?"

"I wasn't emotionally attached to Christopher. There is more at stake with us if it doesn't work out."

"It will work out."

She leaned into his shoulder. "Just hold me."

He wrapped his arms around her. At least she hadn't turned him down completely. Had he asked too soon? He just thought because they spent so much time together that it was enough. She hadn't said no or run away from him. Those were both good signs. But there was a growing ache that told him this could be the beginning of the end. "I will always love you—no matter what."

❧

Will held her hand as he walked her across the street to her house. "Do you love me?"

She squeezed his hand. "Of course I do." More than she knew one person could love another.

"But you won't marry me."

"It's because I love you that I don't think I can."

He stopped her in the middle of the street and shook his head. "That doesn't make any sense. It's because I love you that I want to marry you. If we aren't moving forward toward marriage, then we are stagnant. I can't live the rest of my life like this." He looked up the street and down the street. "Stuck in the middle of the road."

"I like what we have together. I'm afraid if we married, I'd mess everything up, and I don't want to lose you."

"You don't want to lose me, but you don't want me either. I like what we have together, too, but it's natural to want more."

"I'm just not ready to make that kind of commitment. I don't know if I'll ever be."

"What future is there for us if all we have is this? What is the point in continuing our relationship if it's not going to lead to more, to marriage?"

Tears burned the back of her eyes. Was he breaking up with her? "Is it over then?" The words choked in her throat.

"I don't know. I don't want it to be over, but I also can't stay in this place, in limbo."

"What do we do now?"

"Pray?"

He walked her up to her porch and gave her a tender lingering kiss, then left.

She watched Will lumber across the street and put her hand to her mouth as a tear rolled down her cheeks. *What am I to do, Lord?* She didn't want to ruin Will's life, but she also didn't want to lose him.

She schooled her tattered emotions and wiped her tears away before going into the house. She could hear her grandma in the kitchen. She had thought her grandma had gone to bed. "Do you need anything, Grandma?" When she didn't hear anything, she went into the kitchen. "Is everything all right?"

Her grandma had tears on her cheeks.

"What's wrong?"

"Nothing is wrong. Everything is right for once. A few months ago I was a sad, lonely woman spending my last days growing older. Now I couldn't be happier. Thank you for finding me."

She hugged her. "If I had known about you sooner, I would have found you years ago. I don't feel quite so alone in the world with you here."

"Don't forget you have Will. You should count him in your blessings."

She did, but how long would he continue to be in her life now that she turned his marriage proposal down? "Will asked me to marry him."

"I'm so happy for you."

"I didn't say yes."

"Why not, child? He's a good man. He loves you about as much as any man can."

"You didn't marry Grandpa."

Grandma waved a hand in the air. "Don't go using my fanciful ideals as an excuse."

"I don't know how to make a marriage last. I never knew my father, and my stepdads never stuck around. I don't want to live like that."

"You are nothing like your mother. But she raised you a might better than I raised her. I didn't marry Charles because I thought we wouldn't last; I made a choice, a sacrifice."

"Why didn't you ever go back and marry Grandpa?"

"After leaving and keeping his child from him, I had no right to go back. I knew if I contacted him and found out he'd married someone else, it would break my heart. And if he had married but was still in love with me and I showed up, I would want him to leave her for me. I couldn't destroy his marriage that way. I made a choice and had to live with it."

"He never gave up looking for you."

"I know that now. I regret my decision not to go back to him and marry him, but I will never regret having Barbara or you. Your grandfather and I will live on in you. I believe with all my heart that you and Will can make it together for the rest of your lives if you look to the Lord for help." Grandma hugged her. "I'm going to bed now. You believe in yourself. God does."

She watched her grandma pad off to her bedroom. An ache gripped her heart so tightly she held her breath. How sad that her grandma and grandpa had spent their whole lives without the one they loved. Will's declaration bounced around in her head, *I will always love you—no matter what.* She did not want to repeat the mistakes of her grandparents. She loved Will, and he loved her. She wanted to spend whatever days she could with him.

Even though it was late, she swung on her sweater and walked across the street.

His house was dark. Maybe she should wait. Maybe he wasn't asleep yet. Maybe she was crazy for standing in the middle of the street in the dark. Again. This time alone. Then again maybe he couldn't sleep because she had turned him down. She looked heavenward. *What do I do, Lord?* She really wanted to tell him now.

She strode the rest of the way and knocked. When he opened the door, her mouth pulled up into a smile. She definitely wanted to spend the rest of her life waking up beside this man who loved her so much and whom she loved as well.

"Hi?" He was still wearing his clothes from earlier, so he hadn't gone to bed yet.

She could tell by the raise of his brow he was confused by her visit.

"Would you like to come in?"

"Only for a minute." She stepped inside.

"Is everything all right?"

Just seeing him made things right. "I think everything will be fine now."

He pulled his eyebrows down. "I don't understand."

"I don't want to end up like my grandma, alone and lonely my whole life because I let you slip away. I should have said yes earlier. If it's not too late, I'd like to say yes now."

He cupped her face and kissed her several times, then pulled her close. "It would never be too late. I was going to ask you every day until you knew I meant it and said yes." He kissed her for a long time. He finally released her. "I should let you go."

She didn't ever want him to let her go. She wanted to stay in his arms for the rest of her life. All she could do was nod and smile.

"Wait. I almost forgot." He jogged off to his room and back.

He took her hand and slipped on the ring. "That makes it official. You're mine."

And he was hers. She belonged.

A Letter To Our Readers

Dear Reader:

In order that we might better contribute to your reading enjoyment, we would appreciate your taking a few minutes to respond to the following questions. We welcome your comments and read each form and letter we receive. When completed, please return to the following:

Fiction Editor
Heartsong Presents
PO Box 719
Uhrichsville, Ohio 44683

1. Did you enjoy reading *Heritage* by Mary Davis?
   ❏ Very much! I would like to see more books by this author!
   ❏ Moderately. I would have enjoyed it more if

   _____
   _____
   _____

2. Are you a member of **Heartsong Presents**?   ❏ Yes   ❏ No
   If no, where did you purchase this book?_____
   _____

3. How would you rate, on a scale from 1 (poor) to 5 (superior), the cover design? _____

4. On a scale from 1 (poor) to 10 (superior), please rate the following elements.

   ____ Heroine   ____ Plot
   ____ Hero   ____ Inspirational theme
   ____ Setting   ____ Secondary characters

5. These characters were special because? _____

_____

_____

6. How has this book inspired your life? _____

_____

_____

7. What settings would you like to see covered in future
   Heartsong Presents books? _____

_____

_____

8. What are some inspirational themes you would like to see
   treated in future books? _____

_____

_____

9. Would you be interested in reading other **Heartsong
   Presents** titles? ❑ Yes   ❑ No

10. Please check your age range:
     ❑ Under 18   ❑ 18-24
     ❑ 25-34   ❑ 35-45
     ❑ 46-55   ❑ Over 55

Name _____

Occupation _____

Address _____

City, State, Zip_____

North Carolina

3 stories in 1

Unlikely romances unfold in North Carolina. Deidra Pierce seems to have it all—until Eli McKay and his daughter enter her life. Liza Stephens is rescued by a nice guy—then she discovers his real identity. Fun-loving mortician Sharley Montgomery is completely at home in the small town—until Kenan Montgomery rocks her world. Can forgiveness and love find a way?

Titles by author Terry Fowler include: *Carolina Pride*, *Look to the Heart*, and *A Sense of Belonging*.

Contemporary, paperback, 368 pages, 5³/₁₆" x 8"

Hearts♥ng

HEARTSONG PRESENTS TITLES AVAILABLE NOW:

(If ordering from this page, please remember to include it with the order form.)

Presents

Great Inspirational Romance at a Great Price!

Heartsong Presents books are inspirational romances in
contemporary and historical settings, designed to give you an
enjoyable, spirit-lifting reading experience. You can choose
wonderfully written titles from some of today's best authors like
Andrea Boeshaar, Wanda E. Brunstetter, Yvonne Lehman, Joyce
Livingston, and many others.

When ordering quantities less than twelve, above titles are $2.97 each.
Not all titles may be available at time of order.

SEND TO: **Heartsong Presents** Readers' Service
             P.O. Box 721, Uhrichsville, Ohio 44683

Please send me the items checked above. I am enclosing $ _____
(please add $2.00 to cover postage per order. OH add 7% tax. NJ
add 6%). Send check or money order, no cash or C.O.D.s, please.

To place a credit card order, call 1-740-922-7280.

NAME _____

ADDRESS _____

CITY/STATE _____ ZIP_____

HP 5-06